PRAISE FOR ZARA ALTAIR

A cracking yarn that wears its deep research lightly...
— Clarissa Palmer

Leaves you wanting more!
— David Amerland, Author

This series would make an excellent show!
— Joe McGaha, Writer/Producer

If you enjoy mysteries and have a love of history then you have got to check out this book.
— Zain

ARGOLICUS MYSTERIES

Books 1-4

ZARA ALTAIR

Fervent
Crux

INTRODUCTION

Enter the World of Argolicus

With few exceptions, the western world was at peace in the year 512 after Christ's birth. Warlords were plotting in the Balkans either for the East or the West, but mainly for their own power. Rumblings in Persian borderlands perhaps threatened the Roman Empire as seated in Constantinople. The most recent disturbances—betrayals, if you will—of the Frankish kingdoms had been settled some five years. Bishops and clergy squabbled over textual interpretations of the Gospel, patristic writings, or Patriarchal proclamations, as usual, some in a huff, others with conciliatory leanings. Vandals had controlled northern Africa for almost 100 years. The Visigoths ruled Spain and traded with avarice. In Italy, affairs of concern were mainly internal—the parallel Roman law and Ostrogoth legal systems ran under the regal Edicts guided by a sense of civility, providing structure for dispute resolution.

THE ROMAN HEIR

An Argolicus Mystery

LEAVING ROME

The words were not as cold as the Roman winter air, but they stung Argolicus.

"You see," Boethius said, leaning toward Argolicus in a confidential manner, "Rome is a closed community. When someone like you whose family lineage is not from one of Rome's great families and as a newcomer attempts to take on a centuries-old Roman position, you set yourself up for strife. You are wise to retire, go back to your provincial Bruttia, and live as local nobility."

Argolicus watched from the palatial villa on top of the Caelian Hill gentle snowflakes fall on the city and the forum below. He stood on a balcony where Boethius had led him just minutes before. Behind them loomed a grand study filled with manuscripts and books. Boethius carefully peeled an apple, the skin curling off onto the floor at his feet. Argolicus knew everything Boethius was saying, and they echoed his reasons for leaving. He also knew Boethius, so he waited for him to get to the point.

"The same talents that make you a good judge," Boethius continued, "hamper your political power. You read people, you consider all possibilities, you listen carefully to all sides, you weigh outcomes. In politics you must make a decision, move quickly, ignore repercussions, and strike."

Argolicus recognized his political failings and felt the sting of being blocked on more than one occasion by Rome's powerful families and the prelates of the Church.

"Go back to your home, enjoy your studies." Boethius said as he cut off a small section of apple. One of the richest men in Rome, Boethius loved books as much as Argolicus, perhaps even more. "I have a parting gift for you." He bent to the table and lifted a book, handing it to Argolicus.

Argolicus looked down at the small book, almost a pamphlet, but covered in leather.

"I translated it," Boethius said as he looked down at the book. "Aristotle's *Categories*. I know you are one of the few left who read Greek, but I thought you might like it for your collection."

Truly pleased, Argolicus smiled. "Thank you. I will read it in solitude without the endless sessions of reading Greek aloud."

"Ah, Nikolaos," Boethius said, reading Argolicus' mind, "he is a taskmaster." Argolicus' tutor and lifelong companion waited for Argolicus somewhere in the villa.

"He is," Argolicus said smiling, "but without him, my Greek would suffer." The two men stood looking out over a wintry Rome.

"I'm wondering," Boethius said, "Are you going by ship? Or by land?"

"Oh, quickly, by sea. Portus to Squillace."

"Then I'd ask you for a favor."

"Yes?"

"I have another copy for a young scholar. I'm wondering if you could deliver it for me. Books are so precious, I dislike just sending them. Plus, you would like the lad. He loves to read and think."

"Why? Where is he?"

"He lives in Ostia in the old family villa, a large *domus* in the center of the city. His father is a friend of Symmachus, and I thought..."

Ah, here it was politics. Even as he was leaving Rome one last push.

"Of course, I'll take it. We were leaving in four days, but I could leave tomorrow and stop to deliver the book. What's his name?"

"Servius Norbanus Philo. He is the son of Pius."

Argolicus knew this errand tied him to Roman aristocracy, another wealthy and old family. Servius Norbanus Pius had inherited a shipping business that had grown with the stability of King Theoderic's rule. In Rome, his home was near Boethius on the Caelian Hill, but one of the reasons for his success was his constant presence in Ostia near the huge shipping center Portus to oversee the shipping business personally. "Philo," he said. "I shall make sure he receives your gift."

Servius Norbanus Philo met Argolicus in his father's study and office. The young man was lost amid a collection of carved ivory, large enameled plaques, colored glass vases, marble figurines, brass figurines, gold figurines, cast bronze sculptures, tiny enamel boxes, gilt boxes set with gems, silver trinkets, and one elephant tusk displayed on a high shelf. He appeared a very young 17. His dark brown eyes were fringed with long, equally dark lashes. His equally dark hair was cut in the Roman style like a cap around his head, and his olive complexion was sallow with grief and shock. He looked at the book Argolicus had handed to him with a blank stare.

"Boethius is kind," he said in a deep, rich voice belying his slight stature. "I shall write my thanks." He looked up from the book. His gaze slid over Nikolaos, Argolicus' tutor slave, who stood waiting near the entry from the *atrium* next to a large marble statue of Venus. Finally, he focused on Argolicus. "And you are kind to take time to make a delivery in your period of transition."

"Boethius has a way of getting his way," Argolicus said, smiling. "But it was no inconvenience."

"He does," Philo said. "I wish I had half of his persuasive talent because, right now, I'd like to ask your help." He looked as though tears were near.

"My help?"

"Yes. Even I know your reputation. You discover things, you know people, you treat all parties fairly..."

"Philo, I'm flattered by your admiration, but I have left my appointment in Rome. I'm here in Ostia to go home without any title. I have the family estate. I am uncomfortable as it is, intruding on your family when your father was found murdered just this morning. I feel I have no place here."

"There, you see," Philo said. "What if Boethius were asking you for the same request? How would he ask you? My father's been killed, and I need your help. Blood. There was so much blood." He closed his eyes.

Argolicus thought the boy was not as inept at manipulation as he believed he was.

"Why not use the local Promagistrate. Who knows what this investigation will take?"

"He's on vacation in the south chasing the warm weather. The family's left with the local militia. They narrow their activities to apprehension, not investigation."

Argolicus felt the draw of a puzzle, pulled in a breath, and glanced at Nikolaos. "Where did it happen?"

"Right behind your slave, in the *atrium*. I was coming to meet him before he got busy. He said I was too young to go to the games in Rome by myself. I wanted to ask him one more time. It's January, and young people have fun. I wanted to know what it's like to be free for just a few days."

Nikolaos was already in the *atrium* examining the dizzying mosaic pattern on the floor. His middle-aged but lithe body moved as he scanned the expansive floor.

Philo said, "We moved the body and cleaned the floor. He probably won't find anything."

"Where is your father's body now? May I look at it? We can leave my tutor to discover what he will in the *atrium*," Argolicus asked, submitting to the pull of the murder and solving the puzzle. As much as Servius Norbanus Pius was a private citizen, his shipping business kept Rome supplied with goods. Murder was a private family matter under the law, but when it affected the public good, then the Promagistrate instigated public legal investigations.

The young man came out from behind the large table covered in papers and trinkets and appeared to grow in stature and age, separated from his father's large collection. His golden-toned voice resonated among the treasures. "He's in a *cubiculum*."

Philo strode out of the large study, across the *atrium*, and led Argolicus to a small room on the opposite side. Servius Norbanus Pius was laid out on a table, his body was stripped, and slaves were washing with care.

"Ask them to leave," Argolicus said. He crossed the room to the body.

"I... I can't look," Philo said and rushed from the room.

The body was deep pink on top—face, chest, thighs—and white on the bottom along the back. Blood had settled as Pius lay face down on the ground. Argolicus saw five stab wounds in his chest and a large slash across the man's neck. Why didn't Philo mention how brutal this was? Bruises marked his shoulders and arms, spotting purple against the white skin. Argolicus picked up the right hand. The fingers and wrist were stiff, but he saw scrapes and raw patches around the knuckles, and the right palm was slashed. He moved around the table. The left hand was also marked with scrapes but was clutched tight and closed. Argolicus tried opening the fingers to see what was in the grip, but the fingers were too stiff to move. He stood back for an overview, and a sadness at the human condition overwhelmed him as he looked at the evidence of violence.

When he left the room, he found Philo sitting on the edge of the pool in the *atrium*. Tiny snowflakes glittered in the light as they fell into the pool. The pale winter light from the open roof overhead highlighted the youth's body hunkered in dejection. Philo looked up as Argolicus crossed to the pool. "I couldn't bear to see him...like that. White. And the punctures in his skin. The body looked like my father, but it wasn't my father. It was a thing." He stood up to face Argolicus. His face was set and grim, seeming to have lost the sorrow when he first met Argolicus.

"The death was violent," Argolicus said, still in his sorrow for the human condition. "It is hard to see. I've seen more than one. Each time I feel sorrow, guilt, shame for our condition. The first dead body I saw was my father. Although he was not murdered, I remember how I felt. I was about your age."

Philo's eyes widened, and he blurted, "He was? The first dead body? Your father?"

"He was. I know how you feel. I will help you until it is time for me to meet the boat. Maybe, by then, the magistrate will arrive."

Philo looked relieved. "My sister is with my mother. My uncle will be here soon from Portus. My uncle has his own family, but my father was pater familias." He nodded toward a statue near the back wall of the *atrium*, a likeness of Pius fully clothed and looking regal. A slave quietly crossed the *atrium* toward the back bedrooms glancing at Philo.

"I'll talk to them all later. From the state of his body, it looks as though your father died in the early morning. Did you hear anything?"

"No. My room is upstairs." Philo nodded toward the back wall of the *atrium*. "Father's room is downstairs. There would have to be a lot of noise for me to hear something."

"Master," Nikolaos called from the garden. "Master, I have found something."

Philo and Argolicus hurried to the *peristylum*. Argolicus saw the main courtyard, the large pool, columns surrounding the pool, and a garden with many bare shrubs and some small plants surrounding the marble courtyard.

"Over here," called Nikolaos. He stood up in the corner of the room near the other passageway from the *atrium*. "There's blood here on the ground and splatters on the marble."

Philo blurted, "But I found him in the *atrium*."

"We'll look," Argolicus said as he moved toward Nikolaos. Philo followed with a puzzled frown.

"Here," Nikolaos said and pointed to the ground.

Argolicus looked down and saw the blood, now mostly dry, splattered on the leaves of a small plant, on the soil in the ground, and splatters on the marble. He looked to the left and saw the hallway to the servant entrance. "Is that locked at night?"

Philo nodded his head. "Yes, the porter locks it and then goes to his room by the vestibule and the front door."

Argolicus looked at the blood and saw light smears here and there in the *atrium* passageway where someone had tried to wipe up the blood. "Where did you find your father?"

Philo looked through the passageway to the *atrium* and pointed. "Straight ahead, by the *atrium* pool."

As Argolicus followed his direction, a young woman entered the passageway. The first image that came to his mind was a lioness. Her hair was lighter than Philos, backlit by the light from the *atrium* ceiling, it shone in gold highlights. Her skin was honeyed. Her lips and cheeks glowed rose like plump peaches. Her blue tunic, laced with gold cords, revealed inviting curves.

"Philo, are you entertaining a guest, now? Mother wants you."

"Titiana, this is Gaius Vitellius Argolicus. He's come from Rome to bring a gift from Boethius."

Titiana smiled. "Let me guess. A book."

2

FAMILY MATTERS

"My husband had a certain verve for life," Aemilia Atia said. She was a striking woman approaching 50, with handsome features echoed by Titiana, sitting next to her. Argolicus could tell she was used to being in charge. "His brother, Sabinus, is more down to earth."

Aemilia Atia, Philo's mother, had left her bedroom and gathered everyone in the entertainment room when she learned of the guest. The floor was covered in a dizzying array of black and white mosaics, and the walls were painted with intricate scenes of trees and flowers and young people playing musical instruments in nature. Braziers, next to seats, warmed the room from the winter cold. Slaves brought trays of *gustum*: small tidbits of fruit, cheese, and salads for nibbling placed on platters and bowls around the seats, but no one was eating.

"He was a collector. You saw his study. There are storage rooms filled with more. He rotated items so he could enjoy it all bit by bit." She gazed at the wall behind Argolicus. "He had the walls repainted to make them more lively." She looked down at Titiana's clasped hands and placed her beringed fingers over her daughter's. Titiana leaned closer.

Argolicus was about to ask her a question when she continued. "He collected people as well. He worked at developing connections... of all kinds."

Argolicus asked, "Can you think of anyone who would want to injure him?"

Aemelia Atia gazed into a middle distance. "He wasn't always loved. He was ruthless in bargains. But, no. I can't think of anyone who would want to do this." She waved in the direction of the *cubiculum*.

Titiana shifted, her eyes opening wide. "He was..." She stopped, looking at Philo, who said nothing. He sat with the glazed look he'd had when Argolicus arrived.

Argolicus waited, but none of them spoke.

Aemilia suddenly broke from her reverie, "Please, eat. You must be hungry after your trip from Rome. This is no time to lose courtesy. Perhaps it is even more important now." She picked a grape and nibbled off a tiny piece.

Once she had picked up the grape, Philo was the first to reach for a small pastry. Argolicus looked at the array of delicacies on the tray next to his seat: eggs in pine nut sauce, a small dish of asparagus cooked in eggs and herbs, a pastry. He picked up the pastry and took a bite: roasted lamb bits with herbs and pine nuts. As soon as he took a bite, a slave appeared with a light translucent blue glass goblet filled with honeyed wine and placed it on the table next to the tray.

"Father was a busy man," Philo said. "Every morning, he received people here in his study to conduct business. But in the afternoons and evenings, he was often gone. He was very social."

Titiana sighed and pulled away from her mother's shoulder.

Aemilia drew up her shoulders. "He wasn't a family man."

Argolicus waited for more.

Aemilia continued, "He was always out visiting. Sometimes he came home with a new acquisition. He kept the newest ones on his desk so he could admire them. When he arranged dinner parties here, the guests often included new people we had not met before. As exotic as his collection items are... were, he never invited anyone who was not a Roman."

Philo added, "Yes, they had long conversations into the night about Theoderic and his People. He made certain his guests were from old families. They talked about the new appointees from the King. He called them upstarts. They would scheme and plan. But, it was all talk. That's how he and Boethius became friends."

Argolicus once again was glad he was leaving the enclave of Romans. "How do you feel about the King?" he asked.

"Me?" Philo said. "I prefer my books to politics. I have no experience of the 'old ways,' as my father reverently called them. Maybe I'm young. Going to the Games on my own was an adventure for me." He paused. "But I see that it won't happen this year."

Aemilia said, "There will be other years, Philo. Now you are the man of the house. We must make funeral arrangements. You need to learn from Sabinus. You'll be busy now. I'm sure the new Consul, Flavius Paulus, won't miss you at the Games."

"Sabinus?" Argolicus said. The talk was wandering from Pius' death. He felt the time constraint before his boat left. If he could get a better picture of the family, he was certain he would find clues to Pius' violent death.

Aemilia drew up her shoulders and then let them down. "Sabinus is a businessman. An organizer. His life is the port. His daily activities are filled with cargo and the coming and going of ships. He makes certain cargo is distributed to make room for what is contained in the new ships that arrive. He rarely attends social events and even more rarely hosts them. He spends the evenings with his family." She paused. Argolicus saw a tiny frown develop between her elegant eyebrows.

"He is devoted to his family. He has three boys and two girls. He has a penchant for the ordinary and the pedestrian. I've heard him tell the story of Cornelia's jewels in reference to his own children. What can I say? His home is in Portus; his work is in Portus. Pius thought him boring. But, he did make the shipping business run smoothly."

Argolicus waited to see if Titiana or Philo had anything to add, but they were both silent, each seemingly lost in their own thoughts.

"And you?" Argolicus asked, looking directly at Aemilia. "How did you get along with Pius?"

"What do you mean 'get along'?" Aemilia asked. "We were husband and wife. We made things work."

Argolicus waited without responding.

Aemilia shrugged. "We were amicable. I wouldn't say we were a loving couple. We've been married many years. We made it work."

Philo stared blankly. Titiana moved away from her mother and sat primly alone.

"Did you argue?" Argolicus asked.

"Of course, we argued. We were a couple. We had our disagreements, but I can't recall any arguments of any seriousness. Marital disagreements happen with any couple." Before Argolicus could speak, she said, "I don't know who you are trying to ensnare. Philo asked you to look into his death, but I won't suffer insinuations from anyone, especially just the kind of man my husband could not tolerate."

She drew up her shoulders again, stood up, and began to leave the room.

Argolicus stood as well, mentally brushing off her reference to his heritage. "I am sorry I have upset you. Murder is upsetting. I ask questions. The more I know, the better I understand."

Aemilia said, "I'll leave you to Philo."

Titiana stood, glanced at Philo, and then ran across the room. Both of her fists beat Argolicus on the chest. "You don't understand anything," she cried as she hit him over and over.

Philo jumped up from his silent reverie to pull Titiana away.

She turned and sobbed into her brother's shoulder. Then she ran out of the room.

Philo looked at Argolicus. His face was distorted like a young child that is about to cry. "I apologize for my mother and my sister. My father protected them from the world. They feel exposed and defenseless."

"I'm sure they do," Argolicus said. "And you?"

Philo seemed to gather himself. "We are a family. We are not a loving family. My father kept the household running. We all bowed to his will. Even Sabinus. He was pater familias, but at a distance. What my mother said was right. They were married like the contractual arrangement that they made from the beginning. She did his bidding and relied on him for protection."

He stopped. Then he waved his arm at the house before them. "Look at this. Look at all of it. This is a house of things. To my father, people were a means to an end, and the end was things. I was his son, and I was his possession. I must always look good. I'm sure the reason he didn't want me to go to Rome was not because of anything that would happen, but because young people do wild things, and he did not want me to do anything that would reflect on his name."

"And your books?" Argolicus asked. "Did he approve of your library?"

"Yes and no. He approved of the collection. My building my own collection was an extension of his image. But my 'bookishness,' as he called it, upset him. He wanted me to be more of a man."

"A man? What does that mean?" Argolicus asked.

"To be like him, of course. To take the family name out in public. To attend events. To go to parties. To accompany him on his searches for the one new thing. That's what he meant. He cited Boethius as an example of a man who loved books and yet was in the thick of things."

Argolicus had a picture now of the young man's emotional

turmoil. His father was dead, and he had no one to help. He'd been pushed into a position he couldn't handle, and that did not suit his nature. "Ah, to be a man in his image."

"Yes, exactly. My father wanted me to be just like him. I'm not."

"Philo, do you want me to stay and continue? I don't want to upset your mother or your sister."

"Yes, more than ever. You saw how emotional they are. How would they help find who killed my father?" He nodded toward the passageway where Aemilia and Titiana had disappeared. "I need you." He looked Argolicus in the eye.

Argolicus felt an ache at the bottom of his chest at the remembrance of his own father's death. He also remembered the comfort he had taken in the male presence of his uncle, not only a book lover but a maker of books. He nodded.

"Oh, I am grateful," Philo exclaimed like a young child. "I can't make a fancy speech, but I thank you from the bottom of my heart."

Argolicus felt that pain in his chest dissipate. "I will do as much as I can do."

"In that case, I know the perfect room for you here in the house. Let me show you." He led Argolicus out of the entertainment room into the *peristylum* and turned left toward a set of stairs at the far end. "I know it is old-fashioned, but I have a tutor, too. He's probably in my library looking for something for us to read this evening. His name is Bion."

Nikolaos appeared from somewhere in the *peristylum* and followed them up the stairs. At the top of the stairs was a long hallway lined with doorways.

"I like it up here," Philo said. "The rooms have windows. They are light during the day." He led them along the corridor to a door and opened it. Inside the door was a small whitewashed room for Nikolaos and beyond that a brightly painted *cubiculum* set with a bed, a chair, and two small tables. One held a washbasin and small linens; the other was slightly larger to serve as a desk with two oil lamps. A brazier stood near the table against the winter chill. The walls were painted here and there with figures: young women and men singing and cavorting among trees and one lone shepherd playing his pipe.

Argolicus found his travel bag already placed in a corner. "Thank you, Philo. This will do nicely."

"Oh, there is more I want to show you. My library is next door." He nodded his head toward the left. "Once you are settled, I'll show you my collection." His face shown with pride.

"Perhaps after dinner. We can all read together."

"I like that idea," Philo said. "We can read from the new book." He looked around the room and hesitated.

"We'll be fine. I'll arrange my things. Then I'll take a walk and do some thinking. Where will you be in a couple of hours?"

"I'm sure I'll be in my father's study. Uncle Sabinus is due in the next hour. We'll have many things to discuss."

"I'll join you there. I want to speak with your uncle." He watched the young man leave. *Was I ever that vulnerable?*

He must have said it aloud because Nikolaos said, "Yes, Master."

3

NOTHING REVEALED

Argolicus sighed. "I thought I was leaving all this."

Nikolaos looked toward the end of the street. "Just two more days."

They were walking toward the edge of Ostia and the ocean. The streets were lined with empty shops and vacant apartment buildings. For the past 200 years, Ostia had ceased to be a thriving port, the harbor silted in, and what remained was country retreats for rich Romans. Buildings in disuse showed signs of crumbling from neglect. The snow had melted, but a wind from the ocean blew cold, carrying the scent of the sea. Argolicus pulled his cloak tighter.

"I think I would not have liked Pius. Demanding and supercilious. It seems his collection was all he cared about. He didn't seem to care for his family except as an obligation. And the mother, Aemilia, is so cold. I'm sure Pius was a difficult man. But, she paints a picture of a model Roman family. The daughter is right. I don't understand. The boy is the best of the lot."

They reached the end of the street. What used to be the harbor was a silted marsh. Reeds bent in waves as the wind rushed in from the water. They turned and walked along the edge of the marsh.

Nikolaos said, "The daughter, Titiana, seemed overwrought. Hitting you is not a typical Roman action. She's not a child. She looks close to twenty. Old enough to know that what she did is not acceptable."

Argolicus breathed on his cold fingers. "I can't tell if she is upset at the loss of her father or terrified of the murder. Her words 'you don't understand' could mean anything. Did she love her father? Was Pius more strict with her than with Philo? It all seems as muddy as this marsh."

He watched the reeds blowing, lost in his thoughts of the family. He heard Nikolaos turn.

Nikolaos cried, "Hup."

Argolicus turned and began to raise his arms from his cape, but the blow landed just above his solar plexus. Air whooshed out, and he couldn't breathe. He found he was sitting on the ground. His diminutive tutor stood over him, shaking his graying hair.

"Master, you must learn to quicken your response. Even though Romans cannot carry arms under King Theodoric, knowing defense is important."

Argolicus looked up from his sitting position on the ground, took in a couple of breaths, and said, "I don't know which is worse; your endless Greek conjugations or your fight training. Right now, I think it's the training." He took in a few more breaths, then got up. "Time to go back and meet this Sabinus.

✦

Sabinus and Philo were in the study. Philo looked up when Argolicus entered. Nikolaos took his position alongside Venus.

"Argolicus, I was just telling my uncle how Titiana struck you. Uncle, this is Gaius Vitellius Argolicus, ex praefect of Rome."

"Numerius Norbanus Sabinus, Your Sublimity." Sabinus gave a

brief nod tending toward a bow. A short man, in his mid-forties with a gleaming bald dome surrounded by dark curls, Sabinus had the air of a man of business. His tunic was plain but made of finely woven wool. Argolicus saw no jewelry. The man's direct gaze emphasized his erect posture. A man of facts and transactions from head to toe.

Philo continued, "My sister has been distraught lately. I don't know why. For the past couple of weeks, she's been on edge, bursting into tears or blinking back anger for no reason. Father's death has exacerbated her reactions."

Argolicus said, "Everyone reacts differently to death. And murder compounds the feelings. Your sister is young." He decided to lead the conversation somewhere else. He glanced at the desk. "Are you planning the funeral?"

Sabinus answered, "Yes, small. The family only. The priest here will conduct the liturgy. I've arranged for the burial in Rome."

"Sabinus," Argolicus said. "Would you be willing to look at your brother's body with me? To tell me if you notice anything. You saw him regularly."

Sabinus looked uneasy but said, "Yes, I can look. But what do you think I will see? Pius is dead."

"That's just the point. If you could tell me anything, you might notice that is different."

Sabinus nodded. They headed across the *atrium* to look at Pius.

In the *cubiculum*, Sabinus gasped. "He's so pink."

"Yes," Argolicus said. "A disturbing manifestation of death."

Sabinus walked to the edge of the table. "Who would do this? Five stab wounds." He touched each one. "And his neck. Did someone try to cut his throat? This is hard to see."

"Are you alright? It was a vicious killing. "

"Yes, yes," Sabinus answered. "It's upsetting. It looks like Pius and it doesn't. My brother." He bent over Pius' body and sobbed.

Argolicus watched in silence, sensing the man's grief.

Sabinus straightened, touched Pius' face, and turned to Argolicus. "No, I don't see anything that looks different to me."

They turned toward the door and entered the *atrium*.

The doorman, N'Golo, was dark, powerful, and compact as a draft horse, and imposing as though the heavy air of the jungle was wrapped around his being.

"I'm here all night," he said, gesturing to his room off the entry. "No one could get past me. The sound of them pounding in the door would wake the entire household. Look at that thick beam. The doors are heavy. Someone knocks, I open the door. That's how people get in."

"I am not questioning your trustworthiness," Argolicus said. "I'm wondering how someone, not part of this household, could get access to Pius."

N'Golo relaxed his glare. "Why don't you ask the cook, Vasilios? Now there's someone who enjoys being in charge. He lords it over the cooks. He seeks a perfect world unattainable by the rest of us. Ask him because he and his slaves go in and out the *posticum* at all hours of the day and night, bringing in goods and taking out waste. If you are looking for someone who could have left a door open giving access into the house, look no further than the kitchen." He crossed his arms over his massive chest.

Argolicus was soon in the kitchen, where the overwhelming heat of the cooking fires contrasted with the cool winter air in the *atrium*. Dinner preparations were well underway. Vasilios, although not tall, was recognizable from his constant stream of commands as he paced around the work tables. "Don't stop stirring. Small bits, small bits, we're not feeding lions. Stop! Don't put that on until the coals are just right." He noticed the invader, Argolicus, enter the door. "Yes?"

"Vasilios? Could we speak for a few minutes?" Argolicus asked.

"I can't leave. Not even for a moment. Not yet! Wait until the egg has thickened the sauce completely."

Argolicus walked into the kitchen.

"On second thought," Vasilios said, visibly upset. "Let's talk in the corner there by the pantry."

Argolicus joined him at the arched entry to the pantry, where shelves full of urns and herbs towered toward the ceiling. "I'm wondering if any of your staff went out the *posticum* in the early morning."

"Of course," Vasilios answered. "Magda goes out to the fish market when the boats come in. Little Rufus takes the waste to the barges. Gently, gently, Magda. The white fish is delicate. Ali is at the meat market before the butchers. I get the best of everything there is in Ostia."

"Early this morning, who, specifically, went out?"

Vasilios cast his eyes over Argolicus' shoulder."No, no, no. The pasty must sit quietly before it is filled. This morning? Well, Magada for certain. She's preparing the fish now" He grimaced and called. "Demetrius and the martyrs! Rufus, the grapes go on top, not first." He shook his head in a dramatic suffering effect. "You see? I can't leave them for a moment."

Argolicus wondered who had suffered most for the light meal he'd eaten earlier with the family. "Anyone else?"

Vasilios pondered for a moment, his eyes never leaving his industrious workers. "Junia," he called. A young woman left off chopping beets into tiny cubes. "Did you go out with Magda this morning? Ali, prepare another dove, that glutton Sabinus is here."

Junia nodded her head and went back to chopping.

"Just you and Magda?"

Junia nodded again.

Argolicus said, "I'll speak with Magda for a moment. Thank you, Vasilios."

Vasilios nodded as he returned to the work tables. "Peak

under the cloth, Rufus. Those pastries must be ready now. Magda, talk to His Sublimity."

Magda did not remember anything unusual from the morning.

Thinking that talking to people in a group situation was not proving fruitful, Argolicus arranged to interview the rest of the staff, one by one, in his room. He spoke with Bion, Philo's tutor, and also with Pius' ancient tutor, but neither shed any light on the early morning hours. He spoke with household slaves and personal attendants of Aemilia and Titiana. He discovered that the boy, Rufus, had the thankless task of collecting night soil from the rooms, but that happened after the household was up and about. In short, the day's result was dead ends.

⚜

He sat in his room, looking at his notes. "Someone knows something."

"Master," Nikolaos responded, "I agree, but I'm as confounded as you are."

"Well, I am saddened to tell Philo we've uncovered nothing. The person who was closest to Pius, his old tutor Ioses, wouldn't hear an earthquake. His hearing is so bad, he wouldn't have heard Pius leave the room."

Nikolaos chuckled, "Ah, when you are older, you'll have more freedom."

Argolicus raised an eyebrow and smiled. Then his face became serious. "I don't see anyone in this household being angry enough to produce the violence. Five stab wounds. That shows fury, not cold calculation. Sabinus was in Portus. The mother disliked him, tolerated him, but wouldn't want to lose the power. Titiana is hard to read, but I don't see her angry enough. Philo respected him and doesn't seem angry enough, either. A slave or assassin could have been bribed or paid, but then the killing would have been different, not multiple angry stabs, something else."

Nikolaos said, "But it must have been someone he knew. Why else would he meet someone in the middle of the night? And what Roman would be carrying arms, like a dagger, at risk of breaking the law?"

Argolicus looked at his notes from the interviews with the household. There was something, but he couldn't put his finger on it. "It's puzzling. Perhaps it had something to do with his business. We'll go back with Sabinus tomorrow and meet the merchants at Portus."

Nikolaos nodded.

Argolicus rose. "It's time to join the family."

⚜

Bion read, "These are the properties of the rational soul; it sees itself..."

Argolicus, Philo, and Sabinus gathered in Philo's library after a somber dinner. Aemilia had been tight-lipped, Titiana sullen, and Philo submerged in sorrow. Sabinus attempted conversation to no avail. As Bion read Marcus Aurelius, the rationality of the text seemed to sooth everyone in the room. Old Ioses nodded his head in approval of the choice and leaned toward Bion to hear the words.

Sabinus rose, interrupting the quiet flow of words and thoughts. "It's been a tumultuous day. I'm retiring. Philo, sleep well. We'll take care of everything in due course. Argolicus, tomorrow we're off to Portus."

"We are. Thank you," Argolicus said as Sabinus left him with Philo and the tutors. He agreed. What had begun as a mere gift delivery had transformed into a death with no clues in sight.

Philo said, "Marcus Aurelius was so even and reasonable. I'm in turmoil. My father is dead. I'm suddenly the pater familias, and I don't know what to do next."

Argolicus nodded as Bion closed the book and set it aside on a shelf. "Learn from Sabinus. Trust we'll discover what happened."

"Yes, but the politics and the shipping business. My biggest concern was going to the Consular Games and now that sounds so trivial. I need to go among the affairs of men, and I feel unready."

Argolicus replied. "I felt the same way when my father died. You will work your way through the complications. Weeks before he died, my father told me there are two kinds of politicians: the ones who seek the truth and the ones who hide it. I've found if I look to determine what type of man I'm dealing with, I know how to move.

Philo frowned and said, "My father said: secrets flow out of the posticum the way goods come in."

❃   4   ❃

PORTUS

Gray overhead cleared to bright winter sunlight as Sabinus directed his boat toward the harbor of Portus. They entered from a small canal from the Tiber river rather than from the ocean like the big transport ships. The great octagon of protected water, designed by Claudius and completed by Trajan, sparkled as the water rippled under the sun. However much Ostia was a neglected port, the town of Portus and the harbor thrived. Argolicus lifted his palm to shade his eyes.

Ships loading and unloading cargo lined the eight straight sides of the harbor, designed to service the maximum number of ships. Behind the quay, rectangular lines of huge warehouses lined the harbor on every side and beyond. Stevedores scrambled and hauled boxes of fabric and clothing, great amphorae of oil, sacks of grain, and more amphorae filled with wine from ships into the warehouses.

Sabinus pointed to a system of imposing warehouses to their right, filling up space beside one side of the octagonal harbor. "Those are our warehouses."

Nikolaos, who sat at the rear of the boat, gasped.

Two large ships tied up along the quay, masts and spars bare, as stevedores called, grunted, and moved the wares. A tall wooden crane with a pulley attached to a wheel taller than a man was lifting a large amphora from the docked ship as a worker struggled against the wheel. Argolicus watched as their boat neared the quay. The closer they came, the larger the warehouses seemed. Everything here illustrated the family held power and control in shipping goods. Philo was not only pater familias but a rich and powerful young man. Does he realize his political sway? Or, the immense wealth he controls? From his bearing, Argolicus felt the youth did not understand his new position in the world, from son to magnate.

"How often did Pius come here?" Argolicus asked.

"Not often," Sabinus said. "He has a personal storage space here. He came for that. Oh, several times a month. I manage the day-to-day operations. There, do you see that big Syrian?" He pointed to the quay. A large man in oriental dress was pacing back and forth, shouting orders toward one ship, then checking goods as they went toward the warehouse.

"Yes."

"That's Rashad. He says he is Christian, just like you do. But he sees Christ as a man who united with divinity."

Argolicus held his breath, hoping that they would avoid a contentious discussion on the nature of Christ. Sabinus was a Trinitarian, Argolicus by faith followed the Arian two natures of Christ, and now a Syrian Monophysite. He said, "The Emperor Zeno..."

But before he could finish, Sabinus interrupted him. "My mistake. I didn't mean ill. It's just that we know you are of Their Faith. Whatever King Theodoric proclaims, we try to keep remarks on the natures of Christ out of conversations here at the wharf. Our workers come from all over the world."

Argolicus relaxed. Rashad had noticed the boat coming from the canal. He waved and sent two workers over to help tie up the boat. Their boat sat low under the quay. Big transport ships dwarfed the small vessel as stevedores let down a rope ladder. Nikolaos was last to climb the ladder, looking unsettled. Argolicus patted the little man's shoulder. "I see you are getting ready for our journey home." The joke passed by the tutor, who seemed relieved to have the solid stone pavement of the quay under his feet.

"Rashad, my guest for the day, Gaius Vitellius Argolicus." For a brief instant, the big man's green eyes met Argolicus' gaze. Argolicus saw intelligence and hard-edged determination. Then, Rashad dropped his head in a slight bow.

Sabinus continued, "Has The Siren arrived?"

Rashad pointed to a ship anchored in the harbor.

"Good, good," Sabinus said, nodding approval. "Finish with these two, so we can bring her in." Rashad nodded and left to direct the stevedores.

"A good man," Sabinus continued. "He speaks the waterfront vernacular, which seems to comprise words from many languages. I haven't mastered it. I don't know what I would do without him. Well, let me show you the warehouses."

Sabinus led them toward the arched entrance to the largest warehouse. They passed through the entryway with the family name on a marble slab above into a large courtyard. "This is our family warehouse." He led them to a locked vestibule. A slave saw Sabinus approach and began to unlock the door. He unlocked a padlock attached to a bolt at the bottom of a large diagonal timber that crossed the door. He pulled out the bolt allowing the beam to move. Then he pushed the slanted beam across a fitted groove in the floor until it stood at a vertical on the left side of the doorway. The enormous responsibility of warehouse owners to secure the goods stored stunned him.

"Security is our signature." Sabinus continued as they crossed a vestibule, and the slave unlocked a second door. "Pius made sure that everyone knew we take the greatest care to protect merchandise when it arrives," Sabinus said. "A warehouse without security is asking to be robbed."

They entered a large courtyard filled with a black and white mosaic featuring a lion and sheaves of wheat. Sabinus led them across the courtyard to a doorway. "This is the office," he said, gesturing them inside. Two long tables filled the enormous room where clerks sat shuffling papers and ticking off shipping arrivals, storage, and transportation from the warehouse.

"How much of this does Philo understand?" Argolicus asked. The immensity of the enterprise—the ships arriving and departing, the storage, the transportation to destinations throughout Italy—stunned him and would be massive detail to Philo.

"He is learning, but his father wanted him in society, so he has only the barest essentials of how it works."

"So, what will happen now?"

"I can suggest, but Philo must make his own decision on how much he wants to be involved. To him, it seems as though everything came through his father. Because his personality is not... suited... to mingling and politics, I think he would do well here. But he is a novice. My sons know more than he does. Pius pushed the boy model his life in his father's image. When I talked to him yesterday, I realized how little he understands."

A young man entered the office. Sabinus smiled. "Larcius, meet Gaius Vitellius Argolicus. He's the one looking into Pius' death. Argolicus, my son."

Larcius looked like Sabinus but with more hair and fewer pounds. As he smiled, Argolicus realized he had the same open nature as his father. "My uncle," he said and then paused. "Philo will be a different man now." He stopped again and glanced at his father as if he had said too much. "Pater, you know how Pius controlled him. He never had a chance to be a boy."

Sabinus said nothing, but his face showed he agreed. "Larcius, the Siren is in the harbor. Get the bills of lading ready. I'll show our guest around."

Larcius mumbled something, picked up a sheet of numbers, and headed to a large desk table at the far end of the office. Larcius, raised at the port, tackled the charts and tables of numbers spread out around the room.

Argolicus said, "I'd like to see Pius' storeroom."

"Storerooms," Sabinus corrected. "He has three. Follow me."

As they crossed the courtyard again, a slave came at a signal from Sabinus. They walked toward the far end of the warehouse. Sabinus nodded toward a door, and the slave ran ahead to unfasten the bolt that held the locking beam in place.

The richness at the *domus* in Ostia was paltry compared to the treasures in the storage room. Boxes piled high against the wall of one side almost obscured the light from the high windows. Various shades of marble statuary filled the center of the room. Carpets were piled against another wall. Against the third wall, bronzes of every shape seem tangled in a silent battle. One statue of Minerva gleamed in gold from head to toe. Boxes of silver, ivory, gold, and inlaid woods of various sizes crammed together on a series of shelves.

Sabinus said, "He collected things. He collected people. And, he wanted Philo to be like him, but Philo has a different temperament. As much as he tried to please his father, he couldn't fit the mold. Pius was like a bully. Not that he hit the boy or any member of his family, he did it with words—humiliation, judgments of failure. None of them met his arbitrary standards."

Argolicus pulled his eyes away from the treasures. "You say he collected people. What do you mean?"

"Pius did favors for people and expected something in return. Most of the items here in this room, the other two, at his villa in Ostia and his home in Rome, are gifts. He didn't ask for them directly, but everyone understood that a favor, like the Siren being unloaded today before other ships in the harbor, called for a gift. Things arrive here, 'For his Sublimity the gracious Pius from his grateful friend.' They go into the warehouse, and the note went to Pius."

"But, the people. What do you mean he collected people?"

Nikolaos must have overcome his seasickness. He began scribbling notes.

"I'm not sure how he did it, but he seemed to have a hold on people. For some, he would ask outrageous favors, and they were granted without question. If I asked him, he would say, 'You take care of the harbor. I'll manage the politics.' That was as much as he told me. He was my brother but not my confidant. That's the way he was. He took from people, but he shared nothing unless it was in his interest."

Argolicus thought any of a number of people could have had reason to wish Pius out of their life. From no possibilities to a large selection, but where would he start? He chewed his lip for a moment and then said, "Your wife wants us to eat the midday meal at your home?"

"Yes," Sabinus said. "We'll get Larcius. It's just a few minutes walk."

☙❧

"What did you discover?" Philo asked.

"You have a great responsibility ahead of you. Philo, how much did your father tell you about his business connections?"

"Why, do you think one of his connections killed him?"

"It's possible," said Argolicus. "So think. How much do you know about his connections?"

They were in the office at the villa. Philo sat at the desk piled with various stacks of papers. He fanned the edges of one stack, then another, as Argolicus waited for his answer. Philo lifted his head, and his eyes brimmed with tears.

"I tried. I tried. But we were so different. I wanted to please my father. He didn't have friends, he had business relationships. I have friends. A few, but friends. Like the ones who would go to the Counselor Games with me. My father brought people here for dinners regularly, but he met with people other places. He didn't take me with him for those. Look at this." He held up a paper from the desk and read, "Dearest Pius, what you ask is difficult. I thought our arrangement did not include the shipments from Egypt. I do not understand what that means. How do I answer this," he looked at the paper, "Caius Hirtius Lucullus? I don't know him."

"You will get in touch with each of them. As they tell you, you will know what to do. You will determine the ones who seek the truth and the ones who hide it. This business is yours now. You don't have to be like your father. Be yourself."

"I don't know how," Philo answered. His face wrenched with anxiety.

"You do. You will discover a way." Argolicus gave him an encouraging smile. Inside he churned with sympathy for the young man who had inherited a corrupt world from his father. He changed the subject, "Any news of the Promagistrate?"

"No, nothing. Thank you for probing into my father's death. I don't expect you to discover anything, but I appreciate your support."

❦ *5* ❦

SISTER IN THE NIGHT

Titiana startled Argolicus as she slipped past a sleeping Nikolaos and stood in the room. His head was bent over his notes on the small table in his room. He had a list of people he knew were involved with Pius. Under each name, he jotted what he knows. The girl whispered, "My father was a philanderer of the worst sort."

Argolicus composed himself and asked, "What do you mean?"

"He held orgies." Her voice rose above a whisper.

"Orgies?"

"Yes, all those powerful people, he blackmailed them."

If Nikolaos was awake now, he was keeping quiet.

"Powerful, like Boethius?" Argolicus asked. Boethius might be rich, but he also seemed an honest man.

"No, no, no. He didn't go to the parties. It was lesser men. Not consuls and the wealthy but officials—a tax collector, the Promagistrate, military captains, merchants. People like that."

"Titiana, how do you know this?" Argolicus was familiar with young women and their tendency to exaggerate. And, young people often thought the worst of their parents.

"Pacilus. I've had a crush on him since I was eight. Then we became friends, but not lovers."

Argolicus looked at Titiana's elegant face and wondered if she was lying to preserve her Roman dignity. "Why not lovers?"

Titiana paused. Her face betrayed her effort to solve a dilemma. "It couldn't happen... we were friends... friends. We shared our secrets. He preferred men to women."

"I see. He told you this in friendship?"

"Yes. Don't tell Philo. Don't tell Mother. She would never let me see Pacilus again. She's a prude." Titiana wiped a tear from her cheek. Her eyes pleaded with Argolicus. "I think she suspects about the parties but chooses not to know. Pacilus is my best friend."

Argolicus now understood her hesitancy. "I will tell no one." He put his hand on her shoulder.

"Tell me about the parties, what Pacilus told you."

"Disgusting... they were disgusting. My father." Titiana swallowed, then took a breath. Her eyes went from Argolicus to Nikolaos' chamber.

"Don't worry about Nikolaos. He is discreet."

"Well," Titiana began. "He... my father... his friends." She stopped. She brought her eyes back to Argolicus. "I don't know where to begin."

"Tell me how Pacilus told you."

"He came here one morning. 'Let's go for a walk,' he said. I knew he wanted to tell me something important. We walk for the big talks."

Titiana held her hands out toward the brazier as if the warmth could help her tell the story.

"We went down by the marshes. No one goes there."

"I was there yesterday."

"So you know how bleak it is. Suddenly Pacilus grabbed my hand. Tears trickled down his cheek. 'Titi,' he said. That's his pet name for me. 'Titi, I need to tell you about your father.' And then it all came out. My father sent him an invitation. Pacilus was excited. He'd heard about gatherings of important men and felt honored to attend a festivity where he could mingle with important people to enhance his career." Her dark lashes glistened with tears for her friend.

"When Pacilus arrived, the luxury awed him, and the mix of people impressed him. You've seen my father's study. The party was just as elaborate—food, wine, flowers, party favors. He met many important men and other emerging young men like himself. Good families, but not aristocracy. And beautiful young women he'd never met before."

Titiana took a deep breath.

"And then it changed."

Argolicus dreaded what he knew would come next.

"Men disappeared into other rooms," Titiana continued. "With a girl... or a boy. Pacilus found himself with the Promagistrate's hand on his arm. 'Let's see what you are made of, Pacilus.' Pacilus felt uneasy. He has a lover... several. But the Promagistrate? Pacilus felt nothing but disgust once he realized what his intent was. He said he had to go to the latrines and fled. So, that's what he told me... in confidence." She burst into tears.

"Titiana," Argolicus said. "Was Pacilus angry at your father?"

"How could he not be angry? My father invited him on pretense to use him... as a commodity. Another item for his collection. And then he offered him to anyone. More than anything, Pacilus felt Father had betrayed his trust. Pacilus was ashamed. Ashamed that he had been so trusting and naïve. I was the one that was angry. My father had done this to my best friend." Frown lines creased her flawless brow. "Before that, I considered my father distant. But then, after Pacilus told me, I hated him. I hated him with all my heart. As much as I love Pacilus, I hated my father."

She turned her head and looked into his eyes. Argolicus could see the cold hate.

"Would your friend Pacilus take us to this place?"

"We don't need Pacilus. He showed me where it is. I can take you there."

"Yes, let's go first thing in the morning."

Titiana wiped her eyes and nodded agreement.

"I know where Pater kept his keys. I'll take you."

Argolicus wanted more information. Any evil, like decadence, was bound to cause resentment. "Now, tell me more about the men who were there. Did they pay Pius to organize these parties? Or, did they all contribute?"

Titiana opened her eyes wide. "My father did not discuss these matters with me. He kept these activities hidden from the women of the house. Pacilus wouldn't know, either. My father's good name duped him into attending. That invitation..." She shook her head.

"Here's one thing I know. My father liked to own people. He liked to have something on them, have a hold on them. Control, that's what he wanted. As pater familias, he ruled our family. Mother came to terms with him. Her life was here but mostly separate. Philo suffered the most with his sensitive and scholarly nature. Pater did not appreciate those qualities. He belittled Philo. I would do anything for my brother. He is sweet and kind..."

"Titiana, tell me anything you know about the parties. Anything that Pacilus told you. In my short time here, I have a sense of how your father treated his family, all of it. I spent time with Sabinus, his brother. I saw your father's storerooms. Your uncle hinted at the control your father had over the business. Unless you think a member of your family killed your father, I want to consider who would hate your father so much. Who would carry hate in his or her heart strong enough to stab him like that, with force and violence?"

Titiana shook her head again. "No. No one in the family. I

can't believe anyone in the family carries that much hate. Look at my cousin Larcius, so methodical. And Uncle Sabinus he's…"

Argolicus was liking this young woman. Her love of her family and her forthright honesty. But her teenage babbling was preventing him from getting to the point, the real killer of her father. He mustered his patience and said, "Titiana, the parties. Who was at the parties? Of the men Pacilus mentioned, can you think of anyone?"

"I don't know. I know Father had a hold on all of them. I'm a girl. I meet those men on formal occasions…"

"Could you make a list of the men that Pacilus told you were there? That would help me. Unless I knew them in Rome, I wouldn't know the local patricians."

"Oh, yes. I could do that. I'll have it for you in the morning."

As soon as she left, Nikolaos ducked into the room from his alcove. "A despicable man."

"So it seems," Argolicus replied. "I don't know how I will come to any resolution before we leave for home. I'm not sure if going to this hall will help in any way. It will be empty. It's the people I need to know. I don't see how we'll meet those bureaucrats and minor officials that attended those parties in the little time we have left."

"His hidden life," Nikolaos prompted.

"Yes, the people in his hidden life. Even if the girl gives us a list, how can we meet them all and discover anything of depth in one day? It seems impossible. At this point, it seems the best I can do is leave my notes with Philo to give to the Promagistrate when he returns. And, even then, he has total discretion over whether he wants to investigate the killing or leave it to the family. It's a matter of how the Promagistrate interprets his death as impacting the public good."

Argolicus sat in thought. His head swirled with questions without answers. Who were the men? Which one hated Pius the most? How could he discover that? The person who hated him the most might be the best at covering up his feelings.

Nikolaos interrupted his thoughts. "Pius was the most important man in Ostia. Wouldn't that make it a circumstance of public good?"

"Not necessarily. The business will continue with Sabinus, and the commerce is the public good. Plus, the business is across the Tiber in Portus, not Ostia."

"Young Ma... Master," Nikolaos corrected himself. "That puts us in a tight situation. One day. One day."

"Yes, right now, it seems impossible. Perhaps Titiana's list will help. She's an aware young woman. She can tell us about the people on her list."

"Still, one day is a short time. You must put that mind of yours to work."

Argolicus chuckled. "Your opinion of me is higher than I deserve. Titiana's faith in her family is tender, but I'm not yet ruling out the family. Perhaps Philo knew more about his father than his sister thinks. He has reason to resent his father. But hate, I don't see hate. And, Aemilia keeps closed. She is just the type of person I thought of when hate runs deep but is covered by reserve."

Nikolaos said, "But, you should examine that more. She is resistant to your looking into the death of her husband. Isn't that suspicious?"

The lamp on the table flickered. The figures on the wall seemed to dance, but Argolicus felt as though they were mocking his inadequacy.

"This all started with politics and favors. Boethius is a powerful man. It seemed like a simple gesture at the time. One last gesture to the citizens of Rome as I left for home. Deliver a book to a young scholar. Now I've given my word and will fail Philo at a vulnerable time." He slumped in his seat and stared at his notes.

"Master, Philo understands that you did this out of consideration."

"I know how devastated I felt when my father died. He wasn't murdered. It was a freak accident. I can't imagine how murder would affect a young man, a very violent murder."

"Then let's focus on what we can do," practical Nikolaos replied, urging on his master.

Argolicus looked up. "Think of those stab wounds. Deep and multiple. Perhaps, but unlikely. Sabinus could travel back and forth on his vessel and would have access to the villa. We spent the day with him, and he seems to understand his brother's failings, tolerates them, and concentrates on the business."

Nikolaos shook his head. "No, but what about the boys? Not Titiana's friend, but one of the other boys. Is it possible that another boy did not escape the way Titiana's friend did and now harbors guilt and shame?"

"That is a consideration," Argolicus replied. He mulled on this for a moment in silence. "That is a very strong consideration. A young man, strong and harboring revenge. Someone like that could have stabbed in a rage. But how would they get in the house in the early morning?"

They both sat in silence. Argolicus yawned and said, "I thought a friend of Philo's might have got him to open the side door, but then Philo would be awake and wouldn't leave him alone with Pius. No, that makes little sense. It's time to sleep. Perhaps we will wake up with fresh insights."

❧   6   ❧

SEDUCTION AND POWER

In the early morning, Philo discovered them all—Argolicus, Nikolaos, Titiana, and her friend Pacilus—getting ready to leave through the *cubiculum*.

"Pacilus! What are you doing here? Where are you all going?"

Pacilus, a handsome, well-built young man with dark curls and seductive brown eyes fringed with long, dark lashes, stood mute.

Titiana lowered her gaze and then answered before Pacilus could say a word, "Philo, there are aspects of Pater that you don't know."

"What? What are they? Is this about his murder? Where are you going?" Dark circles under his eyes revealed his sleepless night.

Argolicus stepped up to answer. "Philo, your father was not as noble as he first appeared. Pacilus discovered something... dark about your father. We will investigate. One of the unpleasant consequences of a killing is that hidden facts come to light."

"What facts?" Philo asked. "Where are you going? Who..."

"We don't know all the facts, yet," Argolicus answered. "That's why we will examine one of his holdings here in Ostia, a place where he held... gatherings. Parties for certain men."

"Certain men? That doesn't sound factual to me. What parties?"

"Parties for men only," Argolicus said. "And young men like Pacilus."

Philo turned to Pacilus. "You attended these parties?"

Pacilus, looking uncomfortable, nodded. "Once."

Titiana turned to her brother. "Philo. It is time for you to be an adult. I know how Pater treated you. It wasn't just you. He manipulated many people. Come with us. Discover a facet of your father he kept from all of us. Then you will have a new fact."

Philo had the look of a wounded pigeon. He stood still, his eyes focused on some internal vision none of them could see. "I'll come."

Pacilus led them through the streets to an old building that had once been shops but now appeared closed along with several others along the street. Set on the main street, Decumanus Maximus, the building looked as deserted as so many buildings in Ostia. "This is it," he said.

Titiana crossed to the main door and inserted a large iron key. She turned the lock, and the door opened.

Their eyes became accustomed to the dark room lit only by the high windows beside the main door. The plastered walls were painted with figures of men embracing in a variety of positions—standing, sitting, sprawled on beds. Faint scents of perfume, burnt oil, and spices lingered in the air.

Pacilus gestured with his arm. "This is the main reception. The private rooms are behind, and there's a door beyond that leads to baths. Everything I saw here..." He stopped, unable to describe his experience.

Philo asked, "What happened here? I don't understand."

Titiana said, "Philo, take a look at the paintings. Our father held parties here... for men. And for young men. He used his influence to invite young men like Pacilus. Pacilus came expecting honor among men of power in a congenial atmosphere. Instead, it was an invitation to seduction."

Pacilus added, "Philo, there's something you should know about me."

Philo said, "I know. You've been a friend of Titiana's since childhood. I'm not *that*naïve. I saw the signs. You never wanted Titiana. Look at her. She is beautiful. You think I didn't know."

Titiana gave him a hug. "Oh, Philo. You are so discreet. You understand. Pacilus is my best friend. Most girls have best friends that are girls, but Pacilus is mine. I can tell him anything."

Philo said, "You are lucky. I have friends, but no best friend. I wanted to go to the Games with others who were going, but not anyone as a friend. Just company. I thought Father would feel secure that I was with others."

Argolicus brought them back to the reason for the visit, "Pacilus, tell us what happened when you arrived."

Pacilus blushed. "I... I... I was so hopeful when I arrived. A doorman asked to see my invitation. I entered expecting to hobnob with the local elite. Iwas—I still am—looking to advance my political career. I want to leave Ostia and to end up in Rome."

Argolicus nodded, commiserating with the young man's ambition. At the same time, he wanted to go home more than ever to escape the Roman clambering for position.

"He's so good with people. They talk to him," Titiana volunteered.

"Go on," Argolicus prompted. "What happened once you were past the doorman?"

"It was nothing like it looks now. There were lamps and lanterns everywhere. The room was bright with flickering light. Gustum delicacies filled the tables. A fountain of honeyed wine sat in the middle of one table, and slaves circulated with pitchers to fill goblets. Men, and the guests were all men, dressed in finery. Scents from perfumed oils and pomades saturated the air." He paused and took a breath, glancing at Argolicus.

Argolicus said, "I realize how difficult it is to remember and tell us. Any details will help. Did you recognize anyone?"

"Yes," Pacilus said. "Most of the men. They were major citizens here in Ostia or Rome, but here in Ostia for the time."

"Can you add to the list Titiana made?" He reached toward Nikolaos, who brought out a small parchment from somewhere in his folds.

"I'll write them down," Pacilus said as he took the sheet from Nikolaos. "There were a few girls, prostitutes, too. But I don't know their names."

"The girls aren't important. Whoever you remember," Argolicus said. "What about the other young men?"

"I recognized most of them. Some could have been in one of the... other rooms. The private rooms. The rooms where...things happened. Not that they were friends. Ostia is a small town and even smaller when you consider the patricians, most of whom visit from Rome. Pater was one of the few who lived here most of the time. There was Nobilier, he's the son of a military naval officer, and Macrinus—I'm uncertain what his father does, and Arsenius, the son of the Promagistrate, and Otho. His father is a prominent silk merchant."

"Did you talk to any of them? Had any of them been to other parties?"

"I don't know," Pacilus said. "If they had, they probably thought, as I thought at the beginning, that the parties were a step to position and power."

Philo interrupted. "My father! My father did this? Why did everyone know but me?"

Titiana hugged her brother close. "Philo, these are the facts. We have to learn them and know who our father was. You can go home."

"No, I'm staying. Show me the list. Now that Father is gone, I need to know who took part in these scandalous activities.

Knowledge is power just as much as wealth. I will have nothing to do with them."

"Philo, it's not that easy. You are right," Argolicus said. "Knowledge is power. At times, especially in politics—and a small town is almost nothing but politics—that knowledge gives you the advantage. You know of a weakness that those men think is a secret. That knowledge gives you the strength to work with them, to converse, to transact business, to see them in normal social settings. Your anger now may keep you from wanting to see them, but you will soon discover that situations arise when it is better to consider them, to attend to them rather than avoid them. Anything you do here will train you for coping with Rome itself."

"Well, you may be right. But now I am angry." Philo's face flushed, and his fist balled at the end of his slender arms.

Argolicus once again felt his heart go out to the boy. His own introduction to the adult world of complexities after his own father's death was similar but without the grim veneer of murder. "The world of adults is complicated. And politics compounds the difficulties. It's why I'm leaving Rome. I understand. The complications are wearing. I'm going home to avoid those complications."

Philo gave him a grateful look, and his face changed to thoughtfulness. "That's just the problem. You can go home to South, far away from Rome and politics, but I'm here in Ostia with Rome just a few miles away. I have no escape."

Titiana grabbed his hand and squeezed. "Philo, I know you will be a leader. Not in the way father was by manipulating people, but in *your* way. You've inherited Pater's wealth, but not his way of doing things."

Argolicus said, "Wise words from your sister. Now, let's hear more from Pacilus."

Pacilus looked around. "I was at a table piled with snacks talking to a man from Rome, I don't remember his name, when Numerius Sulpicius Asina joined us. The Roman left. That's when…" Pacilus hesitated. He looked at Titiana, who nodded. "That's when Asina put his hand on my arm. He stroked it and said, 'Let's see what you are made of.' That's when I understood the party was not what I thought. He was inviting me to go to one of those rooms." He gestured to the doorway on the far side of the hall. "I couldn't. I just couldn't. I excused myself to the latrines in the middle of the building and then left by a side door." He looked down at the parchment in his hand.

"These men," he continued, waving the list. "These men are not about affection. They are about power over other people." He looked down at the list. "Almost all of them are married and have families. It's not about sexual preference. They want the power of seduction and the influence of secrets. Yes. As humiliated as I was, I'm glad I left. Argolicus, if there's a way I can help you find Pius' murderer, I will. Titiana and Philo deserve to know."

"You are helping now," Argolicus said. "I have today, and then I'm gone. Not everyone would do what you've done—swallow their pride and come here with us. The ordinary exterior appearing as abandoned shops tells me how Pius wanted to keep these parties a secret. Our next step is to examine the list. Add any names you remember to the list. Then, if you want to help more, any of you, help me with reasons any of these men would want to kill Pius."

All three of the young people agreed.

"We've seen enough here. Let's go back to Philo's *domus* and study the list."

Philo and Titiana left to help Aemilia with funeral arrangements. Pacilus added in two names on the list and left for home. Argolicus sat in his makeshift study at the small table in his guest room as he reviewed the list. Between Titiana and Pacilus, there were twelve names in total on the parchment scrap. Twelve names. Twelve men he didn't know. In an unfamiliar town.

He grabbed the parchment, stood up, and called, "Nikolaos, quick. Catch Pacilus before he leaves the *domus*. We need him. I'll be downstairs in the *peristylum*."

When Pacilus arrived in a few minutes, Argolicus said, "I need your help again. If we go to the forum, most of the men on the list will be there. It's morning. Everyone is out conducting business, gossiping, and just being seen. I'm sure it's the same here as the forum in any town."

"That's what it's like this time of day," Pacilus said. "What do you need from me?"

"I need your help to match names to faces. If you could point out the people on the list—discreetly—I'll have a better idea of who they are. Can you help?"

"Of course," Pacilus said. "Any way I can help Titiana and Philo, I am ready."

Argolicus led them into the office where Philo, Titiana, Aemilia, and Sabinus gathered around the large table. The table was clear of trinkets as the four of them poured over papers. Old Bion and Philo's tutor Ioses sat at one end of the table writing invitations to the funeral in elegant cursive.

"I'm off to the forum with Pacilus," Argolicus said.

⚜ 7 ⚜

NOT THE MAN

The bright morning sun did little to ease the crisp air, but it brought what people were in Ostia to the forum. Wrapped in heavy cloaks over layers of clothing, tradesmen hawked their wares beside empty stalls, barbers busied themselves with blades, and the patricians and politicians stood in groups in the center of the large plaza chatting and exchanging gossip.

The empty shops marked only by the mosaic emblems set in the stones in front showed how much the town had dwindled only to serve the few patricians who still came to their country retreats. Argolicus knew he had made the right decision when he noticed the clusters of men talking in the large plaza. He turned to Pacilus.

"If you see any of those men on the list, point them out discreetly. Tell me his name. Mention his position and anything else you know about him. Nikolaos will take notes."

"How will that help?" Pacilus asked.

They passed groups of people and overheard snippets of conversation.

"Ostia will not be the same."

"A vicious murder, I hear."

"Young Philo..."

Talk of Pius' murder was the main topic of conversation.

"I want to know them better. I want of sense of who they are and how they conduct themselves in public." He pulled his cloak tighter as a quick gust came off the ocean. "Is it always this cold here?"

Pacilus laughed. "In the winter." Then his look sobered. "And there you see," he gestured with his shoulder toward three men chatting, "in that group is one Numerius Mummius Paterculus. He has holdings here and a large family villa. He is often in Rome but here in Ostia enough, enough to be part of Pius' circle."

Nikolaos scribbled on the list.

"I recognize him from Rome," Argolicus said. "He loves gossip of any kind."

Before Argolicus could move toward the group, Paterculus called, "Your Sublimity, here you are in Ostia. Come, come. Join us." He was a thin man with a rapacious look to his otherwise bland face.

Argolicus joined the group, introduced Pacilus, and met the other two men.

"Tell us, Argolicus, what brings you to Ostia. Are you avoiding the *hoi polloi* and madness of the Games as we are? Flavius Paulus is a good man, God bless him." He crossed himself quickly but without reverence. "But you know how it is. He isn't a rich as some, and I understand the Games are not a lavish this year...

"I am returning home to Bruttia tomorrow."

A brief disdainful sneer crossed Paterculus' face before he returned to his mask of avid interest.

Argolicus continued, "On my way, I did a favor for Boethius. And now I'm doing a favor for young Servius Norbanus Philo."

"Oh, I heard. I heard." Paterculus said, crossing himself three times as did his two companions. "Such a horror. Who would think it? How fortunate for Philo that you are a magistrate. I remember how you settled that dispute with Velusian's sons. Something about the circus tower and the amphitheater." He paused, hoping Argolicus would fall for the bait and explain.

Argolicus remembered the sons Marcian and Maximiums, how they had lost those items in a drunken gamble to him. He thought of that incident as his actual entry into the adult world. The debt was not recorded. Argolicus had trusted their word, and the sons had petitioned King Theoderic to reclaim their ownership. The matter would haunt him for life. "I'm retiring from the Senate and returning home. Our ship leaves tomorrow. I'm not certain I can help Philo much in the time I'm here."

"Well, you can leave in peace. I hear Numerius Sulpicius Asina returns tomorrow. Although…"

"Yes, it is a family matter," Argolicus said, reading Paterculus' thoughts. He decided to plumb the meddler's knowledge. "Would he help the family even though it's not a public matter?"

"Oh, I know him well. In this case, he might. He and Pius were good friends."

"That's good to hear. Philo and the family will receive support. His murder was quite violent."

Paterculus was all ears, ready for details, but Argolicus cut off his prurient pursuit. "I'm off to find some good vellum to take on my trip. It was good to see you again and meet your friends." He nodded to the three and walked on, Pacilus at his side and Nikolaos trailing behind.

Pacilus said, "What a man. I wonder how I will navigate gossips like that. You do it so well."

"I'm not so sure," Argolicus said. "I find gossips trying. If you learn to observe and curb your responses, it gets easier. Do you see anyone else on the list?"

Pacilus shook his head no.

"Master, now that you mention it," Nikolaos said, "more vellum at good prices is a good idea to take back to the country."

"We'll do that," Argolicus responded. "First, let's see who else Pacilus knows so he can have the rest of the day to himself."

"Do you see those two men next to the big well? They are both on the list. I saw them that night," Pacilus said. "Pansa and Rufus. Publius Hirtius Pansa and Servius Marius Rufus. Pansa's family has been in Ostia for generations. He owns property here and in Portus. He was often at Philo's *domus*. I saw him on my visits with Titiana."

Pansa was a big man, but it was difficult to tell how big because he was swathed in layers of bright silks—blue, green, red, and yellow—topped by a heavy fur against the chill. On his feet, he wore court-style, heavily embroidered soft shoes with crossed straps over the instep. The other man, Rufus, wore an embroidered tunic covered by a wool cape and sturdier shoes with wrappings up to his knee against the cold.

"Rufus is another who lives in Rome but comes to a family villa here in Ostia," Pacilus said. "I know little about him because he's mostly in Rome."

Argolicus lowered his head, wondering how he would greet them without seeming obvious. He strolled among the crowds and, this time, heard snatches of conversation about himself.

"Praetor and then praefect of the city..."

"He must be a friend of the family. I've never seen him here in Ostia..."

"Is he leaving in disgrace...?"

"Those young sycophants of the King..."

His dilemma resolved when Rufus called out as they neared the central well. "Your Sublimity, I see you, too, are avoiding the Games. We are honored to see you in Ostia."

Argolicus approached, shaking his head, "No, I'm going home. I've left the public world."

"But I hear you are helping the family of Servius Norbanus Pius," Pansa said, pulling his fur over the silk layers.

"I am. I was there hours after it happened on an errand for

Boethius, and Philo asked for my help when I delivered Boethius gift, a book."

Pansa continued, "Pius was such an important man here. So many of us respected him. Young Philo must be devastated. Book, you say. You brought a book?"

"Yes, one Boethius wrote himself."

Both men looked at him again. He could see their reappraisal at the mention of Boethius, one of the richest men in Rome. Argolicus had a sense of why they had come under Pius' sway. Riches impressed them.

"Yes, well... an outsider wouldn't be able to help much, but it is a cordial gesture," Rufus said. "Murders are so difficult to trace if done in private. I suppose the family has no recourse but to depend on a kind gesture from someone like you. A man from the provinces. And I hear your mother is one of the King's People. Your father..." He left the sentence unfinished.

Argolicus felt Pacilus tense. Argolicus heard the intended slur and ignored it. He was here to discover what he could about these men. He saw Pansa give Rufus a warning glance.

"Rome has changed," Pansa said, bringing neutrality to the conversation. "We have a King in Ravenna and are left to ourselves here. He doesn't visit Rome. I've been to Ravenna several times. It's full of pomp and regal splendor. The entire palace is a copy of the palace in Constantinople. We Romans have to acknowledge that Rome is not Rome. The Emperor is in Constantinople, and the king is in Ravenna. Most of the goods that pass through Portus go to Ravenna and the north, not Rome. I've heard the great orator Cassiodorus. Isn't he a friend of yours?"

"He is," said Argolicus. "A gifted speaker. We're childhood friends."

Rufus said under his breath, "Aha."

Pansa went on ignoring Rufus. "His laws are fair. He's left Roman law in place for citizens. That doesn't help Pius' family though. The King's People, have a penalty for killing. Even though it is money or something else of value, we Roman citizens must deal with killings on our own. I've heard of your decisions. Often just and usually fair. If you find the killer, I know your recommendations to the family will be honorable."

"Thank you," Argolicus said. "I wonder if you could help me? Do you know anyone who held a grudge against Pius? Any unfair dealings?"

"He was a rich man involved in many transactions," Pansa said. "Too many for me to know. I'm afraid I knew him only as a patrician. I've heard no grumbling about his business dealings."

"He exacted full... he traded in favors," Rufus said. "I won't deny it. In personal business he's not the man many admire. In business there was always a personal favor as well as the transaction. Some became uneasy with his favors. Pius always seemed to come out ahead. But grumbling is not a cause for murder."

Something touched on the truth about Pius. "You are right. Being disgruntled does not lead to murder. Can you think of anyone who had a more powerful resentment?"

Both men shook their heads. Rufus looked up and glanced at Pacilus. "I know you. You're Lucius Mummius Pacilus, yes? You are a friend of the daughter, Titiana. I feel as though we've met."

Pacilus shook his head as his body tensed. "No. I mean, yes, I am a friend of the family. But, as far as I know we haven't met."

Argolicus knew it was time to go. Pacilus was fragile about the party. Much more prying, and the young man might fall into tears or break down in some other way.

"You've been helpful," he said to the two men. "I'm staying at the family villa. If you think of something, anything that might help, send a message. I can meet with you. A visit to the household now is not right. The entire family is distraught."

Argolicus left the two patricians of Ostia and walked toward the market stalls that surrounded the large plaza. Pacilus was silent, lost in his thoughts.

"Pacilus, do you see any more of the men on that list?" Argolicus asked.

Pacilus lifted his head and glanced around the plaza. "No. The others may have gone to Rome for the Consular Games, or they're just not here today." He turned his head to look at Argolicus. "I need to leave. That meeting with Pansa. I was at that party for such a short time. He recognized my face."

"Pacilus, you did nothing at that event. You left before anything happened. We all have a moment when we leave the naivete of youth. Yours was quick with no real dire consequences." He thought about the Roman brothers and their gambling trick. "Mine came much later. Many would have called me a man at twenty-eight, but in some ways, I was more naïve than you. And I had unpleasant consequences. Friends like Philo and Titiana support you. You have the rest of your life. You handled that brief situation well. And, you were right. You hadn't met Pansa. It's just that you saw him at the party."

"You think I handled myself well?"

"Yes. Yes, I do. You will serve your ambition to be in politics. It takes practice. That was practice."

Pacilus smiled.

"Thank you for your help, Pacilus. Nikolaos, let's find that vellum."

❈ 8 ❈

THE PRICE OF NOBILITY

Nikolaos clutched the wrapped pack of vellum sheets under his arm. Argolicus strode in thought along the main road of Ostia, Decumanus Maximus. When the road angled toward the town wall, he continued walking headed for the main gate and the shore of the ocean. They passed the baths and the guild house and working people on the street who served the needs of the lingering patricians. Argolicus was the only patrician on the street as they walked between shops, work-shops, bars, restaurants interspersed by empty buildings toward the city gate.

Argolicus spoke. "There was snow in Rome, but it seems colder here, even with the sun almost at midday."

"No complaining," Nikolaos chided.

"I'm stating a fact. I feel as though it's the only fact I know at the moment. My head is swimming with possibilities about Pius, his family, and his cohorts." He stopped walking, and tradesmen, slaves, workers flowed around him, some giving a fleeting look at his finery, others ignoring the patrician and his slave.

"Master, would you like to stop at a restaurant for a light meal? Perhaps that would clear your head."

Argolicus glanced at the street ahead. Small bars and restaurants sat between shops at regular intervals. "A good idea."

"That one looks quiet," Nikolaos said pointing to an open door ahead.

Argolicus nodded. They found a table inside, and he said, "Whatever looks good."

He sat while Nikolaos left to place an order. A young peasant couple sat at a corner table gazing into each other's eyes. Four workers chatted amiably before the midday break. The rest of the room sat in empty gloom. He mulled over his lack of progress. His offer of help to Philo was coming to no conclusion. He had a better picture of Pius and his manipulations but had met no one who seemed angry enough for a vicious attack in the man's own home. How had they made it inside? It had to be the side door. The big doorkeeper would have known any other entrance.

Nikolaos returned and placed flatbread, an egg, a bowl of steaming lamb stew, and a cup of wine in front of Argolicus.

"I keep thinking it was someone Pius knew well. Otherwise, they would not have access to the house, even the side entrance. The slaves coming and going would have noticed. Aemilia is cold and bitter, but she seems resigned and not angry. Titiana hated her father, but those stab wounds. I don't see her doing that."

"What about Pacilus?" Nikolaos ventured. "We have only Titiana's word that he was more wounded than angry."

"We spent the morning with him. He's more worried about how to pursue a career than hatred. After all, nothing happened. I don't see him like that, full of vengeful anger. I thought about him briefly when Titiana visited, but spending the morning with him, no."

He dipped a piece of flatbread in the stew.

"And those men at the forum. Whatever hold Pius had on them, they were all sycophants at heart. Pansa with his courtier ways without a court. Rufus, with his disdain, ready to belittle anyone. Paterculus and his gossip-mongering. None of them particularly admirable men."

The tangy odors of the stew made Argolicus realize that he was hungry. He ate in earnest. As he savored the stew and tempered the rich spices with pieces of bread, he went back over the morning. The visit to the party site, the people Pacilus had seen there, Philo's shock, the conversations in the forum. Nothing stood out. He was overlooking something important someone had said but did not understand what it was.

"Could it be one of the other boys?" Nikolaos said. He pulled out a note and glanced at it. "Nobilier - naval officer. Macrinus - unknown. Arsenius - Promagistrate. Otho - silk merchant. Perhaps one of them was actually seduced. Didn't escape like Pacilus. And afterward blamed Pius and his decadent gatherings."

"The boys," Argolicus said, slapping his palm on the table. "I knew there was something I overlooked. Exactly, possibly one of them or another young man from another party at another time. A 17 or 18-year-old would have plenty of strength. Even a younger boy who was strong. Let's go back to the villa. Perhaps Philo can help us, at least with these boys."

Nikolaos put away his note and reached for the package of vellum sheets.

Argolicus took a last gulp of wine from the cup, then stood. When he looked around the bar, he noticed the room was empty. The barman stood in the back while voices and clattering came from the kitchen, but the room itself was empty. A silhouette stood in the doorway backlit by the winter sun. A large man entered the relative dark. Tall, but not as tall as Argolicus, dressed in a shabby tunic covered on top by a short leather tunic with no sleeves. A wide leather belt, left over from some military campaign, circled his waist.

The man strode to Argolicus and whispered in a rough hiss, "Do not meddle." He reached out his rough fingers and clutched the front of Argolicus' tunic. He pulled Argolicus close so that his stinking breath flooded the close air. "You are out of your element. The price of nobility is birthright. You are only half there."

Argolicus tensed and growled. "I have a trusted mission. I keep my word."

The man pushed his hand against Argolicus' chest with vigor, let go of his tunic, and turned toward the door. "As do I," he said, striding toward the doorway where he hovered for a moment and then disappeared into the sunlight.

Nikolaos sighed and said, "Master, why did you not fight back?"

"The man was rough, but no threat. He meant no physical harm. The words were a threat." He smoothed the front of his tunic with his palm. "But he was a messenger, not the man or woman who sent the threat."

"Your questions and explorations have unsettled someone."

"Now we need to find out who that is."

When Argolicus and Nikolaos returned, the giant doorman N'Golo leaned close to Argolicus and said, "I think Philo will be glad you are here. They are all in the entertainment room."

From the *atrium*, Argolicus could hear the voices. Among them, he heard Philo and Aemilia arguing with someone. Argolicus headed toward the large room behind the *peristylum* while Nikolaos went up to the room to store the vellum package.

In the elegant room, the braziers burned hot with coals but there was no food. Philo, Titiana, Aemilia, and Sabinus sat while a large man, dressed in silks in much the same manner as Pansa down to the embroidered soft black shoes stood gesticulating. His brown hair was smoothed down over the crown with scented pomade. Heavy, dark eyebrows arched over deep brown eyes. He strode with a commanding bearing as addressed the family, "... because my hands are tied. It's outside the law..."

"Argolicus," Philo said, jumping up a look of relief on his face. "This is the Promagistrate Numerius Sulpicius Asina."

Asina turned toward Argolicus, "Your Sublimity, as you know, this killing, vicious as it may be, is a family matter. There's no way I can help the family of Servius Norbanus Pius. He was a friend. From a legal standpoint, there is nothing I can do. His death is not a public matter."

Argolicus would have to wait to tell Philo about the ruffian or ask him about the boys on the list. He chest ached where the man had pushed him.

Titiana noticed his rumpled appearance and raised an eyebrow.

He gave her a slight nod and turned toward Asina. "Promagistrate, I explained the legalities to Philo when I arrived. The family has money to take up a suit in a court of law, but first, we must find the killer."

"Exactly what I was explaining to them," Asina said. "It is a family matter, they must find the killer to bring suit."

"Perhaps one or two of your men might like to take on a special investigation. I'm sure the family would pay well. Men with families who might want to earn extra money. You could give them a leave. Is that a possibility?"

Asina rustled his silks and took a step backward. He pressed his lips together, paused as if thinking, and said, "These men are trained to quell disputes on the street and other disruptions of public order. They are not in any way investigators experienced in finding murderers. The family would not only be wasting money, they would have no satisfaction."

Asina stood firm on his legal point, and Argolicus wondered why he would not want to find the man who killed his friend Pius. "I see. Is there a man for hire who would do this? Help a family with private matters?"

"Families. My wife died, I have only my son," Asina deflected, then continued with a noncommittal answer "I will ask around. Perhaps I can find someone."

"Let me show you the body," Argolicus said gesturing across the *peristylum* toward the room off the *atrium*. When you see the wounds, you'll understand how this murder was so vicious. We'll leave the family in peace."

Asina hesitated, then stepped toward Argolicus and followed him toward the *cubiculum*. Nikolaos had returned from their sleeping quarters and trailed behind. When they entered the room Pius was dressed in fine silks. The sweet scent of the oils that the slaves had used to clean the body mixed with a slight odor of decay.

Argolicus told a woman sitting in attendance what they needed to see. She shrugged and lifted the silks to expose the wounds. The wounds had turned dark and glistened with the scented oil.

Asina said, "Like battle wounds," as he gazed at Pius' greenish tinged abdomen and the dark maroon stab wounds.

Argolicus said. "A strong arm and great force like the fury of battle. In this case, it was anger. You can see why the entire family is upset and wants to find the murderer. Is there any way you could help his family? I leave tomorrow. I promised Philo I would help, but I have discovered nothing. The more I explore, the wider the circle of possibilities."

"I know Pius and his family. Our connections were often. I suppose most people would call us friends. I'd like to help, but I can't do anything official."

Argolicus said, "That would relieve my obligation. Philo is a friend of Boethius. They exchanged letters. I came here to deliver a book as a favor and this," he gestured toward Pius' body which was covered again. The old woman adjusted folds in the fabric. "The funeral is tomorrow on the island. I wanted you to see the wounds so you would understand how agitated the killer must have been."

"I'll find someone," Asina said. "I'll talk now to Aemilia to reassure her. I'll explain that I can help, but unofficially." He headed toward the door.

"I will tell Philo," Argolicus said as they left the *cubiculum*.

He found Philo and his uncle sitting in the office. The big table was now covered with account books and each of them was pouring over one.

"Philo," Argolicus said standing over the large table. "Asina has agreed to find someone to continue the search. Not a legal search, but a private individual. In some ways, this will be more helpful than anything I could do. A local man will know more about Pius' connections than I do."

"Thank you," Sabinus said. "I don't know why he was being so difficult."

"It was a point of law," Argolicus answered. "Under the law, the matter belongs to the family. Once your brother's killer is found, then it is up to you to bring it to court. I know this is difficult with his death and the funeral arrangements. But now, you will have someone, perhaps two people to help you find the killer."

Philo looked up at Argolicus. "Thank you. I was thinking like a child when I asked you to help. I have so much to learn. I've decided I want to be more like you, patient and thorough."

Argolicus laughed and said, "Philo, it's as I said when we were out this morning, the more you focus on facts, the better you can facilitate your course with other people. I'm flattered and thank you for the compliment, but it's more a matter of experience in life than any special skills."

Philo nodded. "I do. I have much to face. In that way, maybe Pater was right. I need to socialize with others."

"About your father's death, I have no clues. The circle of people keeps widening rather than narrowing. I'm wondering if you could tell me about the boys Pacilus mentioned." He gestured to Nikolaos who pulled the list out of his folds, walked over from the corner where he'd been standing, and handed it to Argolicus.

"And, I want to tell you about an incident we had after we left Pacilus," Argolicus said.

THE CAUTION

Before Argolicus began, Aemilia interrupted crossing the *atrium from* the *cubiculum* containing Pius' remains. Her bearing was as stately as the first day, and her *tunica*, fine green embroidered with gold, but her face was haggard.

"Come," she said, gesturing to another *cubiculum* off the *atrium*.

Argolicus brushed at his tunic where the ruffian had clutched and crumpled the fabric, nodded and followed Aemilia through the door. He signaled to Philo that he would return. The boy looked disappointed but nodded. His mother took precedence.

Vivid frescos of pastoral scenes with shepherds, sheep, flowers, and trees covered the painted walls. The mosaic floor echoed the theme in flowers set among diagonal patterns in hues of green, gold, and a soft rose. Two benches with tapestry padded cushions faced each other set for conversation. In the far corner a chair and writing table were arranged, the tabletop clear except for a sheet of vellum, a pen, and a pot of ink.

"My workroom," Aemilia said as she sat with an erect posture on the other. She gestured to the other bench and nodded to

Argolicus to sit. Argolicus mimicked her posture and realized how uncomfortable the backless bench was.

Aemilia folded her hands in her lap. "I hear you are disturbing things. Your visit to the forum is already gossip everywhere. I don't know how to say this, but you must be more discreet. Your direct and forward manner—I know you want to get to the root of things in a short time—but, your manner has disturbed some important people."

"I feel the pressure to find Pius' killer. I have until tomorrow morning. It's seeming that the more I search, the wider the circle of prospects grows." He stopped, considered her words and continued. "You may be right. In my time as *praefectus urbanus* in Rome, I grew accustomed to assuming authority. Here, I am another Citizen and have no special authority to question much less probe."

"Pius, whatever he may have been to his family, was a leader, perhaps the most prominent man in Ostia. Unlike most of the patricians here, he lived here. The others maintain their places as villas away from the city. They are Romans from Rome. They consider themselves the elite of the elite. But in Ostia Pius was the lion. Because of his position and his manner, he ran this town. I have my reputation as his wife."

Argolicus mused on the decaying and almost empty Ostia. "I understand. Could you help me? I know I asked before, but now you've had time to reflect. Can you think of anyone, young or old, male or female, wealthy or otherwise, who would have reason to be angry, very angry, at Pius?"

"You've been out. You've seen this once thriving port. Pius was just another patrician in Rome, but here he was the leading man. He was one of few who lived here most of the year. Romans who still visit their villas here, bring their household from Rome. They don't keep a separate staff here. This is a town of ghosts and has beens. If someone was angry enough to confront him face-to-face and kill him, it would be someone who does business here—and, if so, they did business with Pius. Kill? I don't know."

"You knew your husband. Did he...Was he...?"

"Did my husband keep other women? Not that I know, and I would have known. Years ago he thought he fell in love with someone, but she turned out to like his wealth more than him. I think that was a lesson he did not forget. I suppose it is possible that some woman killed him out of jealousy, but I find that very, very difficult to believe. He didn't like encumbrances. That included liaisons that required some form of loyalty. No, I don't see it."

"Did he cheat someone out of money or goods?"

"He didn't cheat. He extracted favors. He held power over people with knowledge. If someone asked him to cheat, that was a thing he knew. He wielded that knowledge to gain favors. A very different way of interacting with people than direct deceit in a business transaction. He brought no one to financial ruin. That wasn't his way. The way he worked was indirect, subtle, and always about power."

Aemilia shifted on the bench and leaned forward, her silks rustling with her movement.

"Whatever motivated someone into anger, it was about power, power over someone. It wasn't about business. It was some way Pius cornered someone with his manipulation. I don't know how you will find that person but that's what I can tell you. It's about power over someone."

Argolicus nodded in agreement. "You and your family have been gracious in hosting me here. I leave early tomorrow morning for Portus and then home. Everything that I've learned has only broadened the circle of people I've discovered in Ostia. But instead of narrowing the field at each point the circle gets bigger. I have one more avenue to pursue today with Pius' help. In all honesty, I don't think I'll be able to help your family. I can tell you this. I'm not sure how to tell Philo."

"Philo is my baby, my younger child, but he is now pater familias. In one day he changed from a young man just into an adult and the nominal leader of our family. Learning to handle unpleasant truth is part of that responsibility. He admires you. I see it in his eyes. You are the first man that has gained his true admiration. Oh, he loves Sabinus as his uncle. But, you. You light some spark I haven't seen before. I think he will listen to anything you say, even a disappointing reality."

"I'll tell him when I ask for his help. There's one more possibility."

Aemilia leaned even closer, paused, and then returned to her upright position. "Remember, disturb no more important families. Hints and aspersions to our friends don't help me. Philo is young. Sabinus is, well, Sabinus a good man for business but no leader. Our position has shifted with Pius' death. I'll be frank. I liked my position as his wife. If you disturb the balance at this crucial time, I could lose my importance. I don't want to move to Rome and disappear in a sea of matrons. I like being queen in a small town."

Argolicus said, "I understand your feelings. I made a promise to Philo, and therefore to you. I'll do my best, in the time I have here, to discover who killed your husband. I'll take your suggestion and tread more lightly but I will still probe."

"As long as you understand."

"Which is more important to you, finding Pius' killer or your reputation?"

Aemilia shifted on the bench, her bracelets clinking against her wrist as she put her hand on the cushion. "Oh, now I see why you make people uncomfortable. You ask direct questions."

"I do."

"As long as Pius' killer goes unknown our family lives under a cloud of suspicion. People will wonder what caused someone to stab him. As I think about it, your finding the killer will restore our family name by bringing suspicion and doubt to resolution. Yes, find his killer but go softly."

"I shall do everything in my power for the rest of the day, to uncover the man or woman who killed him." Argolicus paused and smiled at Aemilia. "And, as you instruct, I will go softly. And now I'll find my tutor and then talk to Philo."

⁂

Upstairs in his room, Argolicus found Nikolaos packing the few things they had brought to the villa.

"Master, I was straightening up for tomorrow. I left your things on the table." He nodded toward the table with the pen and the vellum.

"Let's look one more time at everything we have regarding this murder. Where are your notes?"

Nikolaos reached into a deep pocket and brought out his scraps.

"Lay them out on the table. We have just a few hours left."

Nikolaos set the vellum scraps in rows across the table arranging them in order from the beginning to this morning's meeting with the patricians.

Argolicus watched and said, "As of yesterday, we eliminated most of the family. Titiana is the only one left with hatred because of her friend Pacilus. But killing does not seem in her nature. She is rightly angry, and that is all. This morning we met some of the men we know were part of Pius' circle of corruption but not all of them. I just talked with Aemilia and she seems not to know how decadent Pius was. I'm not the one to tell her."

"Why not? You usually tell the truth no matter who it touches or how it touches them."

"On the other hand, I *do* have some sympathy. She's holding on to her position as the matron of Ostia. What good would it do to tell her? She knew he held parties for his friends. Why go into specific details? Otherwise, her sense of Pius is cold and evaluative. She, better than any of the rest of the family, knew how he manipulated people. Let her mourn and be free."

Nikolaos placed the last vellum scrap on the table, then stood back to look.

Argolicus continued, "Aemilia will survive the least wounded. Titiana will harbor her tainted vision of her father. Pius has been shocked into a reality he didn't know existed."

Nikolaos nodded and then pointed to the sheets spread on the table. "We found only some of the men..."

"Yes, and our questioning this morning started a train of reactions. There's the ruffian and the threat. That's straightforward. We need to find who sent him. More unsettling is that rumors have started that I am disturbing the patricians here. Aemilia wanted me to stop searching at all. She felt her position here in Ostia threatened."

"To stop? Stop altogether?"

"Yes, until she realized that finding the killer would lift the shadow over the family name."

"Since the other men Pacilus mentioned are out of town, that leaves only the boys for us. Is that your next pursuit?"

"Something, something doesn't ring true. I can't imagine a boy of Philo's age or even that of Pacilus hiring a man to threaten me. It's possible. Money can buy anything. But it's the act of a mature man, not a boy. That ruffian looked like a man who could go well beyond a mere threat and has done so in the past. If we pushed harder, I'm certain it could happen and in a less public way."

"So, do we forget the boys?"

"No, not at all. I was ruminating. We'll get Philo tell us where we can find them. Bring that scrap. What were their names?"

Nikolaos picked up the sheet. "Nobilier - naval officer. Macrinus - unknown. Arsenius - Promagistrate. Otho - silk merchant. Who knows, they may be out of town, too."

"The Promagistrate is back, so we know his son is here. If he's as burly as his father..." Argolicus realized he was speculating and stopped. "A naval officer, he must be connected with Portus. If they live in Ostia, we're in luck. We don't have time to cross the river again. Otho may be our best hope. His father must serve the matrons here with silks at a cheaper price than in Rome. Let's hope Philo knows Macrinus, and that he is here in Ostia."

"A strange place, this Ostia. It's the center of nothing," Nikolaos said. "The commerce here seems to survive by serving the patricians who still come here."

"I'll be relieved to get home to the country far away from any of the tentacles of Rome and its undercurrents." He sighed. "All this because of a favor to Boethius."

Nikolaos pocketed the vellum sheet. "Shall we find Philo, then?"

❧ 10 ❧

EVERY MAN MUST MAKE HIS OWN DECISION

Aemilia and Asina were talking in the entertainment room as Argolicus and his tutor passed through the *peristylum* on their way to the office. Sunlight fell in an afternoon slant from the open ceiling onto the plants and tiles of the big room. Servants passed carrying food and drink to the entertainment room. Sabinus and Philo were in the office, but they had ceased looking at accounts. Each of them sat in silence staring at the books on the table.

Argolicus told them about the morning in the forum, his conversations with the men, and his disappointment in finding no clues to his father's murder except the encounter with the ruffian.

"But you are describing Asina's man, Altan. Everyone in Ostia knows him and stays clear of him." Philo said, astonished. "When you see him on the street, you know trouble is about to happen. He's not exactly a bodyguard, he's more of a problem solver. He collects debts when they are overdue. I know little about these matters but I hear he settles accounts for brothels when someone hasn't paid or is too rough with a girl. I'm not as naïve as everyone thinks." He turned his young face now marked by dark circles under his eyes toward Argolicus.

69

"Asina's man?" Argolicus replied. "Philo, think. Is there any reason this man Altan, would come to see your father? He is strong," He paused and paced in front of the table. "But he is a mercenary paid to do bidding. One quick stroke would be his way. He appears to know how to do violence, but efficiently. Whoever killed your father was angry... very angry. Those wounds suggest passion, not cold calculation."

Philo started to speak but Argolicus waved his hand to silence him. He continued pacing back and forth in front of the table. Then, stopped. "When did Asina return from the south?"

"Yesterday, from what I hear," Philo said.

"If that ruffian, Altan, is his man, why would he caution me? Does he work for other people? Patricians in Ostia?"

"Not that I know. But, now Asina will find someone for us. He is professional. The Promagistrate finds and arbitrates. His men are trained."

"Was he good friends with your father?"

"He came here for dinners. They did some business together. I just saw here," he pointed toward an account book, "that Father sold him some fabrics straight off the ship so Asina didn't have to go through a fabric merchant."

"That's exactly the way Pius did things," Sabinus said. "He would tell me to pull certain items from the warehouse. And, that is how he made friends. He gave favors and expected them in return. It's how he grew and maintained his power."

Argolicus rubbed the sore spot on his chest, remembering the grab and the threatening warning. "Let's go see him. He's with your mother."

A tray of *gustatium* snacks accompanied by honeyed wine now sat on a table in the entertainment room between Aemilia and Asina. Titiana sat by her mother's side.

"... and so you won't have to be involved. These men will work to find..." Asina was saying but stopped when Argolicus, Philo, and Sabinus, trailed by Nikolaos appeared in the archway. The Promagistrate twisted with a questioning look at the group.

"Ah, Asina. You haven't left. I had a question," Argolicus said.

"Yes?" Asina's face was blank of emotion.

Aemilia glanced at Argolicus to caution him not to push.

"I'm piecing together a chronology. When did your ship arrive?" Argolicus said, moving into the room. Aemilia frowned at him.

"My ship? My original ship was to arrive yesterday. But I tired of the provinces and returned three days early. Why do you ask?" Asina stood as Argolicus moved into the room.

"And did you see Pius when you returned?"

"Yes, yes, I did. I sent a messenger to set up a meeting, and he came to my house." Asina paused as his eyebrows squeezed together. "We met, we talked. He..."

"And your meeting was successful?"

"We came to an agreement. We..." Asina paused again, pressed his lips together, and shook his head back and forth. "No, we disagreed."

"You disagreed about your son, Arsenius? You were upset."

Asina stood still. His pupils enlarged, darkening his deep brown eyes. He sat down and stood up. Aemilia and Titiana leaned forward as Philo and Sabinus moved closer to Argolicus.

"Arsenius?" Philo said startled. Titiana looked up with recognition as her eyes met Argolicus.

"Yes, Arsenius," Argolicus answered. "Your son, Asina. Your son told you something while you were away. He told you something that made you hurry back to Ostia."

"Arsenius," Sabina said, shifting in his seat as his voice broke. "My son. Pius. My friend, Pius. Because of Pius my son lost..." His hands tightened into fists at his side. "My son, he seduced my son. Arsenius will never be the same. That is not friendship." He sat and put his head between his hands. "I came in behind the slave with the fish. There was a boy. I asked him to find Pius."

"What are you saying?" Philo asked, his young eyes gleaming out of the dark circles. "You came here to harm my father? You, the same man who tried to seduce Pacilus, Titiana's friend? You hypocrite."

"I made a choice," Asina said, his body losing its authoritative bearing. Everything that had been tight slackened. "Arsenius had no choice. He was beguiled, forced. Pius, your father, told him if he did... if he... Pius told him it was nothing, the physical act. He told Arsenius that he would sponsor him. That of all the young men in Ostia..." Asina looked as if he would cry. Then he took a breath, closed his eyes, and sat still.

Then he leaped up. "Yes. Yes, I killed him. That liar and seducer. I was there to confront him. Pius came out of his room and we met in the *peristylum*." He gestured out toward the big room. "He made the same argument as you, Philo. But, my son, my son... had no choice. Every man must make his own decision. He said in time Arsenius would understand and that I would understand. I said it was rape. It *was* rape. Insidious mental rape first, then the physical act. That's the way Pius dealt with every-one. He twisted thoughts and made every bargain come out in his favor, even a young man's virginity."

"And the knife?" Argolicus asked. "Romans are forbidden by law to carry weapons. Only the King's people carry weapons. You must have come with thoughts of murder."

"It was night, I was on the streets alone. Who would notice?" Asina said. He sat down again. "We're far from Ravenna. This is a Roman town. I don't know if I set out to kill him. I wanted to confront him. Killing him could have been in the back of my mind. I was angry. I wanted amends. But when he started with his excuses of power..."

Sabinus interrupted, "We will strip you of everything. We'll take this to court and win unequivocally. Our family will have justice." He pulled Philo next to him. "Look what you have done to this boy. He's distraught with grief, overwhelmed with discoveries about his father."

Aemilia sat stock still, her face composed in Roman dignity, and said, "Asina could be anyone Pius touched." She signaled to a slave, "Get N'Golo to show this man out." She folded her hands in her lap and watched Asina crumble into his silks in front of her.

Titiana rose and pulled the stunned Philo toward a bench. She wrapped him in sisterly arms as he stared out at the middle distance.

⁂

Argolicus and Nikolaos readied for the ship to Squillace in southern Italy, long before the family was up for the funeral. But a haggard Philo met them in the vestibule as N'Golo was removing the large bar on the door to let them out. Philo opened his mouth to speak and instead rushed to Argolicus, embracing him.

Argolicus put his arms around the young man and then gently pushed him back.

"Find the facts. Think about them first, putting your emotions aside. Use them to your advantage."

Philo nodded.

"Know yourself and trust your sense of justice. You will be a man much different from your father but your own man."

Philo looked at him with trust in his eyes. "Thank you. Thank you. Without you... I've learned so much. You are welcome in our home always."

Argolicus picked up his bag and nodded to N'Golo. The big man pulled open the door. Nikolaos slipped out into the predawn gray. Argolicus said, "*First say to yourself what you would be; and then do what you have to do.* Epictetus said that. I'll send you a book."

THE USED VIRGIN

An Argolicus Mystery

WELCOME TO ANOTHER TIME

Enter the world of Argolicus.

With few exceptions, the western world was at peace in the year 512 after Christ's birth. Warlords were plotting in the Balkans either for the East or the West, but mainly for their own power. Rumblings in Persian border-lands perhaps threatened the Roman Empire as seated in Constantinople. The most recent disturbances—betrayals, if you will—of the Frankish kingdoms had been settled some five years. Bishops and clergy squabbled over textual interpretations of the Gospel, patristic writings, or Patriarchal proclamations, as usual, some in a huff, others with conciliatory leanings. Vandals had controlled northern Africa for almost 100 years. The Visigoths ruled Spain and traded with avarice. In Italy affairs of concern were mainly internal—the parallel Roman law and Ostrogoth legal systems ran under the regal Edicts guided by a sense of civility, providing structure for dispute resolution.

POLITICS NO MORE

Argolicus was finished with Rome and its rumors, innuendos, and back-handed back stabbing. He was finished with politics.

At home and retired, he was enjoying the afternoon sun at his estate in Squillace in the far south of Italy. He gazed at the tranquil bay of the Ionian Sea beyond the harbor. Trade boats bobbed in the water waiting to carry oil, wine, cattle, or horses up either coast to Ravenna or Rome. A lone horseman cantered up the road from the bay. From the kitchen, he heard voices and murmurings as his mother held her daily counseling for the slaves. Perhaps someone was pregnant, or a grandfather's hips hurt too much for him to walk. Close at hand Nikolaos was reading aloud from Herodotus expounding on the origin of Egyptian gods. Soon it would be Argolicus' turn to read aloud to his lifelong tutor and receive the usual slight corrections to his pronunciation.

It was a deceptive false spring day in Februarius. The sun was out, the sky blue, light puffy clouds floated across the sky in a gentle wind. Green grass, herbs, and shrubs covered the landscape. The horses, sheep, cattle and goats grazed and browsed soaking up the sun. In the pruned vineyards he thought he saw light shining through a few red leaf buds. Let those Roman patricians suffer in the snow. This was the place to be.

Nikolaos continued on about the possible origins of Zeus and Herakles and the belief systems in Athens and Egypt.

A sudden clattering on the stones of the courtyard jerked him from his doze. He had just enough time to compose himself before the doorman came through his study out under the portico to announce, but there was no announcement. A tall young man with very intense blue eyes rushed past the slave to greet Argolicus.

"Ebrimuth!" Argolicus immediately recognized his childhood friend by his intense blue eyes. "How is your estate, your Third?" He asked with a smile.

The man was about his age of early thirties, a Goth but dressed in a Latin tunic. He was just as large as Argolicus and towered over the doorman who had been robbed of his traditional protocol. Their fathers had been friends and somehow he was related to Argolicus' mother, but he wasn't sure how. Now both of them were fatherless, just over thirty years old, and making their way in southern Italy.

"The estate is quite prosperous, thank you. I heard you had returned from Rome. I am so happy to see you after your years in Rome," he enthused in the Gothic language. "Have you returned to bring *civitas* to the south?"

Argolicus chuckled. "I have no such intention. I'm here to run the estate and take care of my mother. Perhaps I will find a new wife. Do you know of someone?"

"No, not that I can think of." Ebrimuth paused and then continued. "But I need your help. Rather, my neighbor Adeodatus needs your help."

"I'm a little rusty on the farm matters but I'm certain Nikolaos can find something in his herb garden to help. Is it a mare having trouble? A goat whose milk has gone sour?"

"No, no, no. Nothing like that. This is serious." Ebrimuth

turned his blue eyes to gaze far out across the sea. "It seems impossible, but it is true."

"Ebrimuth, what is it?"

He paused, fiddled with the belt around his tunic, gulped and then stated, "Adeodatus has been accused of raping a virgin."

Nikolaos looked up from his book. The doorman who was retreating stopped still. Silence filled the small garden.

"Adeodatus?" Argolicus was stunned. Adeodatus was renowned as a conservative who imitated the old Roman virtues trying in a slightly judgmental way to bring culture and civility to a south far from Rome. Argolicus had quick flashes from childhood: a sling-shot, a wounded rabbit, Adeodatus sending him to make amends, meeting a sobbing Julia who later became his wife, and having the courage to tell her he had wounded her pet. Adeodatus had taught him responsibility and justice from an early age. No wonder he had been his father's friend.

"But this is unthinkable. Even politicians in their most evil intent refrain from this accusation. It is like deliberate murder. It is so black an aspersion it taints the accuser. Who could make such a claim?"

"Well, that is why I came to see you. There is no normal recourse. It is the Governor himself, Venantius, who made the claim and holds him prisoner."

"I've retired," Argolicus claimed with a sigh. Nikolaos folded up the book.

❧ 2 ❧

THE HORSE TRADE

On the inland road the next morning, Argolicus along with Nikolaos who went wherever he went and Lucius, the estate overseer who was a fine judge of horses, plodded along on three horses under the unseasonable warm winter sun.

"Do you think Ebrimuth understands that I really have no power, no official capacity?" Argolicus asked his tutor.

"He knows that you are retired. He understands that you will use observation and judgment as you did as praefect."

On the pretext of needing a breeding stallion for the estate, they were on their way to the local governor's estate.

Venantius was the son of Liberius but Argolicus had never met him. He remembered tagging along with his father to visit Liberius who arranged for the distribution of the Thirds to all of the Goths and was renowned for his fair dealing. He remembered an old man, but everyone is old when you are five. He remembered many trees.

They topped a steep hill. Argolicus looked out over an expansive estate—villa, barns, stables, outbuildings, fields— which covered the opposite hill. Horses grazed in various pastures or stood in small groups under trees. As far as he could see everything was neat, well-ordered, and in good health—animals, plants, fields, trees.

Venantius turned out to be anything but old. He stood by the paddock on a low wooden podium in a silk toga woven in an intricate and colorful eastern pattern. He was much younger than Argolicus, perhaps twenty and gleamed with youth and beauty. His hair was cut so that his brown curls tumbled about his head heedless of the smooth fashion in Rome. Behind him was a table laid out with cups and small plates of silver tended by two servants who dispensed wine and *gustum* of fried squash, olives, mushrooms, cheeses and bread at the slight wave of Venantius' hand. Venantius was commenting on the next stallion.

"Now, this one is from the same line your father bought some years ago. We keep records of all the horses that leave, especially the stallions." He spoke to Argolicus but it was Lucius who would make the decision. Argolicus' idea of a good horse was one that went a long distance with smooth gaits, comfortable.

Lucius was silent so Argolicus followed his lead. Venantius gestured several times more for other horses to enter for viewing.

"Well, if that one doesn't please I've saved the best for last. Bring in Mercury's Flame." Venantius motioned to the handlers. Chestnut was too mild a word for the gleaming red color. The horse gleamed red in the sun. He pranced around the paddock shaking his head. If beauty was any criteria this was the horse. And if beauty was any criteria, Argolicus thought, the horse was more beautiful than Venantius. The stallion didn't have to try, he just emanated strength, conformation, and elegance.

Lucius nodded. The handler brought the horse over. Lucius leaped over the paddock fence and went inside. He ran his hands over the horse talking some nonsense that Argolicus could not understand. The horse nudged Lucius with his nose. Lucius looked at Argolicus. This must be the one Argolicus read in his eyes.

The two overseers haggled through the bargaining while Argolicus ate lunch with Venantius on the terrace: stuffed dates, pheasant in wine and plum sauce, puddings of fruit, local wine from the vineyard which was known throughout Italy. Argolicus noticed that in spite of all the puffery about keeping records Venantius was just as happy to have his overseer strike a price as Argolicus was to let Lucius make an offer. Clouds were rolling in from the sea. He found the boy Governor's conversation trivial. In spite of the horse buying ruse, he was no closer to finding Adeodatus. At the moment, Venantius was going on about wines from the various vineyards and who was using which processes and what results they were having.

"...and in southern Lucania the soil is even dryer so the grapes..."

Venantius paused mid-sentence as Lucius and the overseer approached from the barns. Both whispered—the overseer to Venantius, Lucius to Argolicus. Venantius smiled. Argolicus tried not to frown.

"Nikolaos," he called. Nikolaos came from the kitchen looking quite sated with the lunch. He pulled out a sack from inside his tunic. Argolicus counted out the appropriate coins.

Mercury's Flame was waiting along with the other horses by the paddock. The sun was hidden by a towering cloud. Argolicus felt he had learned very little about Venantius except that he was self-centered and self-indulgent. He did not know what he would tell Ebrimuth.

The farewells were brief. Lucius mounted the stallion. The extra fourth horse was tied behind Nikolaos. Argolicus mounted and turned toward home.

"Young master, I need to tell you what I learned in the kitchen," Nikolaos said.

From behind the cloud, lightning flashed. Argolicus hoped it would be a dry storm.

"Nikolaos, 'Master' will do. I've been of age some time now."

Thunder broke over them in a roar. The stallion shied then twisted. Lucius was in the air. The stallion bolted and Lucius was on the ground. Argolicus heard shouts and hoof beats as he struggled to control his own horse in the confusion.

"...and even though some claim that the land in Lucania produces the sweetest wine, we all know that the grapes grown right here in these hills are the best in Italy." Everyone at the table nodded in agreement with Venantius. Except, Argolicus. He did not know enough about wine and grapes and vineyards and soil and sunlight in combination.

Evening arrived before the horse had been collected and a veterinarian found to deal with Lucius' shoulder. Venantius insisted that Argolicus stay overnight and that Lucius have a room of his own so that he could rest with the sling-like contraption the veterinarian had placed over his shoulder. He was in the room now sleeping away after drinking some poppy juice mixed with sweet herbs.

Argolicus was disappointed. He had hoped that with the longer stay he would discover more information about Adeodatus, but all he had experienced was a long and boring dinner.

The guests for the evening, a family from a nearby estate, lounged around the table. The father, Gaius Scipio, his wife, Julia, and their daughter, Valeriana. The family had no hint of Rome about them.

The father wore his best but plain tunic, the mother wore some intricately wrapped hair style that was out of fashion when Argolicus was a boy, and the girl, about 14 or 15 years old, was in a modest long blue tunica with a bit of embroidery around the neck. They seemed like honest country folk. Only the daughter wore jewelry. The simple gold links spaced with pearls were no match for Venantius' dazzling rings and hammered gold bracelet.

Julia, the wife, spent most of the evening gazing into the middle distance. Valeriana alternated between aggressive pouts and obvious boredom. A single musician strummed a lyre in a cubiculum off to the side.

Venantius did most of the talking during the meal. Argolicus noticed that Gaius Scipio and his wife made few comments, and those were of assent. Argolicus was tired from the events of the day. The dinner seemed endless but now, finally, they were picking at the honey custards and the end of the evening was near.

Gaius Scipio spoke up. "I've been thinking about the new lands and wondering if we will have enough slaves to tend the vineyards."

Venantius gave a quick glance at Argolicus. "Now, now, Gaius," he placated. "All in good time. We don't want to bore our guest recently arrived from Rome. I am certain dinner conversation there is much more sophisticated than our humble country concerns."

A grunt and a squeal came from the other side of the triclinium. The daughter, Valeriana, stood up covered with wine. Her cup lay on the table. Wine dripped on the floor. At once her parents were on their feet. Gaius Scipio made apologies to Venantius. Valeriana's eyes met Argolicus' with a look he could not read. She ran from the room crying.

Gaius Scipio shrugged his shoulders, "She's been unpredictable lately."

"Don't worry," Venantius replied. "I am certain it is just a stage. I was young once."

Argolicus refrained from raising an eyebrow, much less laughing.

A servant appeared with a lantern to lead the guests to their rooms.

The cloistered musician ceased playing. Rain spattered on the roof and fell to the courtyard in rivulets. Lightning flashed somewhere in the distance.

"Ah, peace at last." Venantius leaned back and motioned for more wine.

Argolicus looked through the opalescent blue goblet in his hand. The glass was delicate and very thin. He wondered how it kept from breaking. He speculated on the cost of an entire set.

Aloud, he said, "One of the things I learned in Rome was how precious the quiet moments are."

Venantius nodded.

"I enjoy being back. Visiting neighbors is a good way to get reacquainted with Squillace. I appreciate your welcoming here this evening."

Another nod. Venantius was definitely feeling the effects of the copious amounts of wine he'd consumed throughout the evening. His eyelids hung heavy.

"I was looking forward to seeing Adeodatus, an old friend of the family, but I hear there is some trouble."

The eyelids fluttered up. Argolicus thought he saw an involuntary twitching but he was not certain.

Venantius sobered. "Ah, yes, Adeodatus. I suppose you want to hear about that."

Argolicus nodded in his turn.

"Who would believe that self-righteous prig would take advantage of a young girl? It was the very Valeriana you met this evening. The one who spilled the wine."

Argolicus remembered the unfathomable look she gave him before she ran. "It's no wonder she's "unpredictable" as her father called her. What an unsettling experience."

"He was visiting Gaius Scipio to buy a horse, just as you are here. As Gaius Scipio tells me, Adeodatus cornered the girl in a hallway and enticed her into his room. She woke the entire household with her screams. Adeodatus was caught almost red-handed. When the servants arrived he was in his room and somehow fully dressed. The girl was crumpled in the hallway unable to speak. She just sobbed. Well. Gaius Scipio sent a messenger here. We retrieved Adeodatus and he is now imprisoned. No threat to any virgins at this time."

"He's here?"

"Yes, and suitably imprisoned."

"I would like to visit him."

Venantius' face shifted. "He's allowed no visitors. That is part of his punishment."

"But surely, an old family friend."

"I have decided. He has no visitors. No family. No citizens. No one." At last, Venantius showed an aspect Argolicus had suspected all along.

"Well, that's that then." Argolicus said, thinking nothing of the sort. "It's been a long day. Perhaps someone could show me to my room."

$$\text{❦} \quad 3 \quad \text{❦}$$

THE SEARCH

The servant handed a lamp to Argolicus and left him at the door to his room. He was tired, fairly cranky, and took complete affront at Venantius' arrogance. He was too exhausted to check on Lucius. A good night's sleep and he knew he would wake up with an answer to what to do next. Somehow he would find Adeodatus.

In the room shadows leaped in the flickering lamplight. The young women in the wall fresco seemed to sway and the trickling from the outside rain brought life to the water pouring from the pot one held as it flowed to the basin below. The geometric patterns on the mosaic floor flashed light and dark in the wavering light. The entire room seemed alive with movement except for Nikolaos curled on the floor asleep, gripping his stylus.

He was so still that for a brief moment Argolicus thought his beloved tutor was dead. But Nikolaos murmured and stirred. His hand gripped the parchment and his eyes opened.

"Young Master." He smiled. Argolicus was so relieved he did not correct him.

Nikolaos got to his feet and glanced at the parchment in the dim light. He went around the room lighting one lamp and then another.

"There is someone here. I think it could be Adeodatus. As we ate in the kitchen the overseer came in with two workers... big fellows. The cook filled up a pot from the soup on the fire and the two men left. The overseer gave the cook a wink and then went into the house. I was sketching a map of the buildings I could remember..." He held out a small parchment, then picked up his stylus from the floor.

"Nikolaos, let's put our heads together and fill out the map and then search for Adeodatus." The two of them marked buildings, barns, outbuildings, corridors with squares and scratch marks. Thunder rolled outside and another bout of rain burst from the sky.

"As long as the rain keeps up, we'll have time to find him." Argolicus was relieved. Now he could hope to find Adeodatus and discover why Venantius was punishing him. He still could not believe that Adeodatus had raped a young girl. He would defend his father's friend.

"There are the barns, the storage granges, the stables. Look, we remember five smaller outbuildings. They must be for tools and tack for handling animals. Then there is this larger one far out by the vineyards. I'm certain he's in one of the outbuildings."

Nikolaos said, "There are storm lamps in the pantry by the kitchen. I'll go to find one. If anyone asks I'll tell them my master is hungry." He winked and slipped off down the hallway.

Alone Argolicus thought about Venantius. He was young, spiteful and self-centered. He did not care if others were bored by his long ramblings about wine production, vintages, vineyard care and the like. Argolicus could certainly imagine him being just as selfish about human dignity and even human life.

Nikolaos slipped back into the room. "I think one lamp should suffice." He pulled the lamp from the folds of his tunic and held it up.

They bundled their cloaks around them against the storm. Nikolaos lit the lamp and then pulled down the cover. Argolicus followed Nikolaos—he seemed to know the way—down the dark hallways until they came to a side entrance. The cloudburst had stopped for the moment. Nikolaos lifted the cover of the storm lamp. The dim light shone out on a sea of mud beyond the paving stones.

Argolicus stepped off into the mud. His feet sank into the ground and mud clung to his shoes.

"This will take some time," he whispered. Nikolaos nodded.

"Master, those two men were big."

Argolicus looked down at his diminutive tutor. "We'll think of something."

They trudged away sinking and slipping in the mud toward the first outbuilding.

The storm lamp cast little light. The clouds seemed close and blackened the sky. They weren't really able to look at the small sketchy map they had drawn in the room. Argolicus tried to remember all he had seen during the day when they were looking at the horses. The stable to the right, a barn behind, the large building out by the vineyard. Where were the others? They couldn't just stumble and slide around in the dark mud. They had to search systematically. But if they went everywhere surely someone would see them. He wasn't looking forward to meeting two big and antagonist men. He was bigger than Nikolaos but his fighting skills had rusted during his time in Rome. Plus, he'd never really excelled in military arts.

Their plan seemed ridiculous—walking around in the mud in the dark without knowing where they were going. Plus, they really didn't know if the prisoner was Adeodatus. And why had he let his loyalty to his father's friend lead him on this wild goose chase? He slipped and fell on his knee.

"Master," Nikolaos whispered.

"It's alright. I'm fine. But, perhaps we should turn back."
There, he had voiced his thought.

"If we go back without looking, what will we tell Ebrimuth?"

They trudged on slipping through the sticky ooze of mud.
The first outbuilding was by the stables and held tack and other
equipment for horse handling. Up the slope and blessedly less
muddy was the barn. At the near end was a lean-to filled with
large pitchforks and other instruments for animal handling. At
the far end of the barn was a shed with small doors opening along
the front at chest height. Argolicus delighted that the mud was
not as deep hurried in the dark toward the shed.

"Master, no."

"I won't stop until I know we have looked everywhere for
Adeodatus." He opened the door.

He smelled birds and heard an enormous cackling and rustling
of feathers. A large and strong buff-colored bird launched feet
first against his shin gouging him just below his muddy knee. The
birds made a horrendous din that hurt his ears. He backed out
and slammed the door. He leaned down to massage his leg.

"Master, they are the fad among the rich country folk. They
are called chickens."

"We will never have them at my place." He tried to wipe the
mud off his leg so he could see the wound. Blood oozed down his
leg leaving a track down his muddy shin. Nikolaos made a small
noise. Argolicus looked up. "What?"

"You've been away from the country too long." Nikolaos burst
into muffled laughter behind his hand. The lantern bobbed.

Argolicus looked in the jiggling light of the lantern. His leg
was a mess. His cloak sagged with mud. Sticking to everything
were hundreds of tiny down feathers from the birds.

"Devil birds," he muttered. "How could anyone think of such
hideous things as a prestigious fad?" A cow in the barn started
lowing. "Let's get out of here before someone comes to check on
the animals."

As he spoke, a door opened in the slave quarters and women's voices carried up the hill. Two lights glowed as they advanced. Nikolaos closed the storm lamp. Argolicus and Nikolaos scurried behind the barn. The women headed up to the chicken coop. When they opened the door to check, the noise started up again. They closed the door and, chatting and laughing, headed back down the slope.

"There one more place to look. The winery." Argolicus said.

"Off we go." Nikolaos opened the lantern again and they headed up the hill.

Thunder rolled in the distance but when Argolicus looked up the clouds were breaking. He saw a few stars. The ground was covered in grass. As they walked, the grass scraped mud off his feet with every step.

As they approached, the winery loomed dark and large. It was built into the side of the hill on the edge of the vineyard. The complex was large, larger than the villa. They skirted the slave quarters.

Amazingly the big double main doors were not barricaded. Argolicus held his breath waiting for a squeak as he pushed at the right side door. Not a sound. The hinges were well-oiled. Obviously, the slaves were kept busy in the off-season.

An overpowering scent of grape must assaulted his nose. The room was like a large cavern. In the vague light of the lantern, Argolicus could not see a ceiling. In the center of the room, huge wooden timbers stood tall with ropes swinging from various pulleys attached. In the middle, an even larger timber like the trunk of an old oak tree jutted out at an almost horizontal angle.

"He can't be in here. If he's here at all it will be in another room."

"Master, be careful."

Too late, Argolicus felt a sound thud to his forehead as he bumped into one of the poles keeping the big turning log in place.

"Stay by me. See, there." Nikolaos held up his lamp. Next to the great wine press was a large rectangular hole in the floor for stomping the grapes. "You don't want to fall in."

"By Demetrius and all the martyrs, this place is a death trap in the dark. Let's get to the other side."

They found an archway behind the large press. Nikolaos lifted the lamp. The scent of fermenting grapes was stronger here than in the large press room. Across from them was a large room filled with amphorae neatly arranged with labels tacked on the wall: *mulsum*, *turriculae*, a small stack of *carenum*, and other labels obscured by darkness.

To the right a long and broad hallway led to various archways opening onto rooms for processing and storing wine.

"This isn't promising," Argolicus said.

"Let's look more, Master."

Argolicus spotted two doorways at the end of the hall. Wooden doors closed off the rooms. They hurried down the hallway almost choked by the musty smells. Across one doorway a large wooden bar blocked access.

Argolicus heard a moan, then, "Just let me die."

"Here, here." Argolicus motioned to the wooden bar. Nikolaos set down the lamp. Together they lifted off the bar. Argolicus opened the door.

The stench was overpowering. It was not fusty grapes but human excrement. Stacked around the room were baskets for harvesting grapes. Argolicus heard another moan.

On the floor behind the baskets in the far corner of the room, a man lay on his side in a pool of muck—excrement and blood. What was left of his tunic clung to his body with clots of blood. In front of his face, a dirty bowl held leftover food. His hands were tied in front so he would have to lap at the bowl like an animal. His feet were tied with a rope which led to a ring in the wall. He moaned. Argolicus took a step forward.

"Adeodatus? Adeodatus."

Adeodatus blinked open one eye. The other was swollen shut. "Argolicus? But what are you doing…"

"Let's get you out of here." Argolicus bent to untie the ropes. "Nikolaos." Nikolaos set down the lamp and began untying the knot at the wall ring.

Adeodatus began crying and mumbling incoherently. "So young…I didn't…I didn't…She tricked…Screaming."

Argolicus murmured as he worked the rope. "Don't worry. It's all over." He freed the rope. "We'll get you out of here."

"I think not," a voice behind him boomed.

Argolicus and Nikolaos turned and stood.

Nikolaos was right. The men were big. The one who spoke was dark, tall and wide with tremendous shoulders. The second was red-headed and taller than the door, perfectly formed but huge.

"What are they called again, Rufus?" The first one asked.

"Chickens."

"Yes, well we found our chicken." He stared Argolicus in the eye. "It wasn't hard. We followed your trail of feathers."

As the first one's arm came out for a punch, Nikolaos cried, "Hup. One."

Argolicus immediately put his weight on the balls of his feet and brought his arms up. As he saw Nikolaos fly by toward the red giant, he dodged the first blow.

Underneath the arm of his opponent he brought is fist up from his waist and hit hard to the middle of the man's higher abdomen as Nikolaos had taught him years ago. Argolicus danced out and back beyond the big man's reach before the big one could recover. The man threw a wild hit toward Argolicus' shoulder. It glanced off. Argolicus went in under the arm again and, this time, brought his arm up from below straight at the man's chin.

He glanced beyond the big brown one. Outside the door, Nikolaos was attached to the giant. The tutor was pulling the giant's red hair and hitting with something. Argolicus saw blood on the floor.

His chest hurt, all the air went out of his lungs, and he fell back all at the same time. Harvest baskets tumbled around him. He thought he heard Adeodatus moan. But, it wasn't Adeodatus. He moaned.

Anger surged through his body. He pushed the baskets away just as the big one was leaning over to deliver a punch. Argolicus grabbed his hair, yanked his head down and kicked him in the groin.

❊ 4 ❊

A BATH AND A LETTER

Argolicus and Adeodatus sweltered in the *caldarium*. Nikolaos dabbed at Adeodatus' face in the places he had nicked while cutting off the filthy beard and shaving him. Adeodatus, covered in purple, yellow and blue bruises, was telling them his story.

"That Valeriana! I don't know how they convinced her. She is so young. I'm certain they promised her jewels and a good marriage. She stood outside my room and started screaming, 'Help! Rape! Help!' I came out of the room to see what was going on. She gave me a wicked smile, ripped open her tunic and cried, 'Rape! Rape,' at the top of her voice. I didn't understand until Gaius Scipio appeared with those two big brutes. I recognized them immediately. They belong to Venantius. That's fine Nikolaos, you may stop. He calls them bodyguards but really they do all sorts of dirty work and bullying around the countryside. When Gaius Scipio sneered and the two brutes grabbed me I knew. Venantius and Gaius Scipio want my vineyards."

"What? Your vineyards?" For the time of a blink, Argolicus couldn't quite believe what he was hearing. Then he thought about Rome and destroying a man's reputation to gain his property made sense. "It was all a ruse, then?"

"Yes." Adeodatus sighed and his spirit seemed as fragile as his old, bruised body.

"You never touched the girl?"

"No. Me? With a fourteen-year-old virgin? That's absurd. It goes against all principle."

"Yes, well, I thought as much. That's why I'm here."

Voices and the clumping of wooden sandals erupted from the *tepidarium*. Venantius, surrounded by slaves burst into the *caldarium*. The two battered brutes trailed behind.

"So, the great praefect of Rome has found the noble Adeodatus."

"Yes, and Cassiodorus knows I am here."

Venantius lost some of his threatening pomp. "Cassiodorus? And so? I am the governor of Bruttia."

"Ah, but he is the King's right-hand man. And my best friend since our childhood."

"Then, how...?"

"Oh, politics, of course. Although it will not be good for you, or Adeodatus. Any of us."

"We know whom we know," proclaimed Venantius, Governor of Bruttia. He turned with a rustle of silks and clumped away on the wooden clogs trailed by his retinue.

Early the next morning Venantius, anxious to see them gone, had a cart filled with feather-stuffed sacks to carry Adeodatus and Lucius. He loaned a horse to pull the cart and a rider for Mercury's flame.

Valeriana came out to the courtyard. She gave Argolicus another unreadable look then rushed inside.

The afternoon sun cast a soporific lassitude over the garden. The first bees buzzed in the flowers. Adeodatus droned on in excellent Greek as Herodotus explained the customs of the Taurians.

Argolicus watched the old man read. The bruises were turning green and yellow, the cut on his head was just a red seam. Adeodatus looked up from the book and smiled first at Argolicus and then at Ebrimuth who was there to take the old man home after supper.

Down the hillside, a messenger rode up the hill. Argolicus was ready for the message but was anxious about the consequences. He had, as he'd promised Venantius, written to Cassiodorus. Cassiodorus would then present the situation to King Theodoric. The answer was from the King.

"A messenger," Argolicus announced to the group. Adeodatus stopped reading and tensed. They all watched the messenger's progress.

They waited in anticipatory silence until the doorman brought the messenger out. Argolicus accepted the message tube. When the messenger was gone he lifted off the top, reached in, pulled out the rolled vellum sheets, broke the seal, and unrolled two sheets.

The first sheet was a note to him from Cassiodorus, the King's Secretary and Argolicus' lifelong friend.

"Most Dearest *Mus,*" Argolicus began reading aloud. "Although the circumstances are peculiar and our most treasured King was not in the best of health…" Argolicus stopped reading aloud. "Ah, this is a note to me." Everyone leaned forward as Argolicus quickly scanned the note.

One phrase stood out. *Your friend Adeodatus will not be pleased.*

He looked up and glanced at all of them: Nikolaos, Ebrimuth, Adeodatus. "We will read this together," he said.

"The crimes of subjects are an occasion for manifesting the virtues of princes. You have addressed to us your petition, alleging that you were compelled by the Spectabilis Venantius, Governor of Lucania and Brutii, to confess yourself guilty of the rape of the maiden Valeriana."

Everyone looked at him and nodded in agreement.

"Overcome, you say, by the severity of your imprisonment and the tortures inflicted upon you, and longing for death as a release from agony; being moreover refused the assistance of Advocates, while the utmost resources of rhetoric were at the disposal of your opponents, you confessed a crime which you had never committed."

"Yes, yes," murmured Adeodatus. Tears welled at the corners of his eyes.

"Such is your statement. The Governor of Bruttii sends his *relatio* in opposition, saying that we must not give credence to a petitioner who is deceitfully seeking to upset a sentence which was given in the interests of public morality."

"Public morality!" scoffed Argolicus. "I'm sorry, I shall continue."

"Our decision is that we will by our clemency mitigate the severity of your punishment. From the date of this decree you shall be banished..."

"What, banished?" Adeodatus cried. "I'm too old for long journeys."

"Let me finish, please, Adeodatus," Argolicus grumbled.

"...And on your return no note of infamy of any kind shall be attached to you; since it is competent for the Prince to wipe off all the blots on a damaged reputation. Anyone who offends against this decree, by casting your old offence in your teeth, shall be fined three pounds of gold."

"There is more, but it is just Cassiodorus closing."

No one spoke. Adeodatus began to weep.

Ebrimuth got up, walked over to Adeodatus, and put a hand on the old man's shoulder. Adeodatus immediately burst into loud sobs.

"Here, here, Adeodatus," Ebrimuth consoled. "Come with me to Burgundia. I have some business with grape vines."

Adeodatus stopped sobbing and looked up at Ebrimuth. "I don't know what to say. I am confused. I must go lie down for a while."

Nikolaos rose, took Adeodatus by the elbow and guided him inside.

"Ebrimuth, do you really have business in the north?" Argolicus asked.

"I do." He stood up to leave then frowned. "It's shameful, just shameful, to treat an honored man that way. I'll go home now and get ready. I will pick him up tomorrow in the early morning. Don't worry, I will take care of him."

"Thank you, Ebrimuth. If it weren't for you, he might still be languishing in that winery...or worse. Even so, Venantius has friends at court."

Ebrimuth took his leave.

Argolicus was left alone in the afternoon sun. He looked out over the ocean sparkling blue in the distance. He saw the messenger start down the road after a meal in the kitchen. The fields on either side of the road were covered in spring wildflowers. A slight breeze whispered in the trees.

"Politics." Argolicus sighed.

Behind in near the barns a rooster crowed for no reason. Now Argolicus recognized the sound.

THE VELLUM SCRIBE

An Argolicus Mystery

ARRIVAL

The patrician, Argolicus, dropped his practice sword when he heard his mother cry out. He ran from the courtyard to villa's front, followed by his sparring partner and tutor slave, Nikolaos.

A cart stood in front of the villa at the end of the road that came up from the town of Squillace. The Ionian sea shone blue in the early morning March sun. The carter unloaded several wooden boxes, carefully placing each one on the ground. Argolicus heard his mother laugh and saw her long blond braid covered by thick arms. A large man in a plain brown robe held her close in a tremendous hug and then pushed her away.

"Uncle," Argolicus cried in Their Language. His face broke out in a spontaneous smile.

The big man turned. "Argolicus. The Father and the Son together!"

"Worship and glorify," Argolicus responded. "Uncle Wiliarit, where have you been this time?" He embraced his uncle, who reciprocated in a hearty hug, squeezing him into the large chest.

Wiliarit continued in the language of The People, "I've been in Constantinople working on a commission. But now I'm here to finish, and I'm hoping Nikolaos will help."

Nikolaos heard his name and came closer, still clutching his practice sword. Besides keeping Argolicus in practice with arms, he was an excellent grammarian and had taught Argolicus Greek since childhood. But, his language skills stopped at the tongue of King Theoderic and his people.

"Nikolaos?" Argolicus replied.

"Yes, it's a medical reference book. He knows much about plants and herbs. I'm hoping he can point out some live specimens for illustrations. What I have now as a source are drawings in another manuscript. I want this one to be as excellent as possible. It is quite a large commission."

* * *

Argolicus put down his pen and knife and looked up from his calligraphy of The People's language when he heard Nikolaos calling his name outside the villa. Wiliarit, his uncle, had chastised his nephew for not practicing writing and had set him to calligraphy with the language of The People—the king's People, Wiliarit's People, his mother's People, his People. He glanced down at his work and frowned at his lack of skill. Wiliarit was right. Neglect was obvious.

But now, Nikolaos was closer, and his calls were urgent. "Master! Master!" He arrived panting in the study.

"What is it? I thought you were looking for flowers." Argolicus said, standing up from his table.

"We are. We were. But down in the Angel's Meadow, there's a body. Come." Now, his tutor was out of breath.

"A body? Do you mean someone is dead? A dead body?" Argolicus shook his head.

"Yes, yes, a very dead body. His face is blue. The skin..." His face distorted as he searched for words and then gave up. "You must come and see."

Argolicus nodded, reached for his cloak on a chair, shouldered it against the cool late March air, and followed Nikolaos along a maze of animal trails over a hill to a verdant meadow. Here and there, wildflower colors - yellow, purple, blue, red - protruded among the green of early grasses.

Wiliarit stood in his dark brown robe in the middle of the meadow, ignoring his unopened box of paints and vellum sheets beside him. His head was bowed, and his arms uplifted in prayer. They waited for him to finish. When he concluded, Wiliarit lowered his arms, raised his head, and turned toward Argolicus.

"Alone... without a burial." Wiliarit shook his head. "And his head—who would do such a thing?"

Argolicus walked toward the body. Dark hair covered his head, but the skin was dark blue. Mottled arms of orange and red skin tones poked out from an old linen tunic. A wool cloak lay crumpled under the body. The odor of rotting flesh permeated the cold air. Argolicus noticed the concave wound on the skull and knew the cause of death.

"Days," he said. "He's been here many days. A week? Maybe." Sunlight glistened off a ring submerged in a bloated finger—a circlet of gold with one dark ruby. "I know that ring." He turned to Wiliarit. "Do you remember Lucas?"

Wiliarit nodded. "Yes, so sad. That was a hard lesson for you."

"Lucas? The son of Bartholomaeus?" Nikolaos asked. "That Lucas?" He moved closer to Argolicus and the body and peered down.

"It wasn't his fault our friendship ended," Argolicus said. "It was his father. His father didn't want him near a heretic like Wiliarit. Remember all the antagonism toward Our Church and the threat Wiliarit posed to his son's true faith? Father was a Roman. With Father, a Roman, gone, Wiliarit's influence was anathema. The Nature of Christ is always a contentious point, especially here in the South. Lucas came one last time to say goodbye even though his father forbade his seeing me."

"He was a better swordsman than you," Nikolaos said. "But what is he doing here? Why doesn't his family miss him? I've heard nothing about his being missing among the slave gossip."

Argolicus stood. "We must tell the family. Nikolaos, go back and tell Lucius or whoever is in the stables to get horses ready."

"I'll stay here by the body and paint," Wiliarit said. "As I remember, I would open old wounds. That would just add to the old man's sorrow."

"Closed minds seem to stay closed," Argolicus said. He sighed. "We wouldn't want to open those old wounds now." He turned toward the disappearing Nikolaos and shouted, "Two horses. Just two."

Wiliarit looked at his nephew. "I know you are a grown man now, but do you think it is wise to see that family?"

"They have to know about Lucas. Being direct is always the best action in the long run. I'll deliver the news and leave."

Wiliarit nodded. "Go in peace. I'll just sketch that little red flower. I've forgotten what Nikolaos said it was, but he can tell me later."

***

"What do you mean, Lucas?" Bartholomaeus asked. A man in his late fifties, his voice filled the room as he glowered at Argolicus. His face was long, accented by a prominent hooked nose. "In Angel's Meadow? He's in Rome, or he was leaving Rome to visit a monk in the mountains. Someone named Benedictus. You must be mistaken."

Argolicus stood in the *atrium* of the large villa of Vibius Horatius Bartholomaeus, whose money supported the local church. The midday sun shone through the opening above onto the rich mosaics on the floor and highlighted the man's silk robes. His biblically named sons, Matthaeus and Marcus, stood next to him cast from the same mold—dark hair, sturdy medium build, and a permanent frown. The surrounding walls were painted in bright colors and frescoes of saints, richly adorned, but saints. Argolicus knew even though he was equal in standing, religious affiliation to the Trinitarian doctrine held more power here than it did in Rome. Not all Christians were equal here, no matter how much King Theoderic had proclaimed tolerance and cooperation in his rule of *civilitas*. This family held the local power because they supported the Church. But, whatever the staunch religious antagonist had to say, Argolicus knew Lucas was the dead man in the meadow.

"I recognized his ring. And even in death, I recognized my friend," he said, keeping the topic focused on the dead body and not religious debates.

"Stop. Stop right there. He is... was... not your friend. Get out of my house with your barbarian tricks." Bartholomaeus put up his hands as if to ward off Argolicus. His gesture denoted abhorrence rather than an order to leave.

"I will leave here to notify the bishop, so the man will have a burial. He was bludgeoned with a club or large branch. He deserves Christian care."

Bartholomaeus scowled.

"Father, Argolicus is right," Marcus, the younger son. said. "Our first concern is to care for Lucas." He turned to his sister, Maria, dark-eyed and lithe. "Get people ready to receive his body. We will prepare him here."

Maria looked at Marcus, then her father, and gave a tearful, beseeching look to Argolicus before she turned to find the servants. Her soft leather shoes padded across the marble mosaics as she headed toward a hallway.

"Our bishop, Braga, will serve all of our funeral needs," Matthaeus said, his frown an echo of his father's dark glower. "Now, you can leave." His silks whispered as his arm swept the air in a dismissive gesture toward the entry.

"Matthaeus, wait," Marcus said, stopping his brother. "I will go with Argolicus to bring back Lucas." He turned to Argolicus. "I'll meet you in front. I'll bring slaves and a cart."

Argolicus took in the three men and nodded at Marcus. "Your Sublimity," he said to Bartholomaeus. He turned toward the entryway and strode across the grand room to the vestibule. Nikolaos trailed behind.

In the vestibule before the large entry doors, Maria emerged from a small room. Once again, her brown eyes implored. "Wait," she said. "I want to talk to you. They are lying." She pressed a small folded piece of vellum in his hand and scurried away.

When Marcus arrived outside, he rode alongside Argolicus as Nikolaos and a cart with six slaves to load the body trailed behind. His bearing was not as aggressive now that they were away from the villa.

"You have to understand that my father's faith keeps him from seeing the big picture."

"My friendship with Lucas is part of that big picture he missed," Argolicus said. "I know now that people come and go in life, but Lucas was a friend, a part of my youth."

"Your friendship started my father's disapproval of Lucas. My brother was always a bit of a rebel, and Father wanted to quell his differences."

"His differences? When we were together, he was a normal boy—running, climbing trees, shooting arrows. What is different about those things? You are supporting your father's ideas without looking at what was happening. We never once talked about religion. We were boys exploring the world." Argolicus felt his anger grow as he tightened his grip on the reins. Marcus was an adult. Why didn't he form his own opinions?

Marcus shifted in the saddle. Nikolaos behind them and the slaves on the creaking cart all were silent in the way that collected gossip and then sent it everywhere.

"It was your uncle. After your father died," Marcus paused to cross himself, "Your uncle came to stay. Father was horrified at the prospect of a monk of your faith influencing Lucas. Lucas was heartsick when Father cut your connection. It was as though his youth stopped then. He became withdrawn. He didn't share much of what he was doing. His presence was like a black cloud. None of us were sorry to see him go when he left for Rome."

Argolicus felt sorrow grip his heart. He had lost a playmate and friend. At the time, his family and his friend, Cassiodorus, Senator, had filled his life. Lucas had found no people to fill his life. Instead, he had drawn away.

They rode in silence toward the meadow.

THE BODY AND THE SOUL

The wagon full of slaves creaked to a halt in the meadow followed by Marcus, mounted on a horse. Wiliarit turned toward the wagon with a somber face and began putting his brushes and paint pots into his box. The midday sun warmed the meadow air. More wildflowers had opened, sprinkling colors throughout the emerging green grass. But, the odor of the decaying corpse filled the meadow.

Marcus dismounted and inched up to his brother's body. He looked, bolted back, and then turned, vomiting over the fresh flowers in the grass. A slave ran up to offer him a cloth. He wiped his mouth, took a deep breath, and turned back toward what remained of Lucas. He stared open-mouthed gasping for air. He crossed himself three times and then raised his hands, palms up, and began to pray. "Blessed is our Lord God, always; both now and ever, and to the ages of ages."

The slaves around the cart raised their hands and stood mute as they listened to his prayer until the end when they joined in to recite, "Lord, have mercy," twelve times. Marcus put down his hands and looked at Lucas' body.

"His face. His face," Marcus said. "It's dark as a devil. Is this what happens when the soul departs?"

Wiliarit opened his mouth, but Argolicus frowned, waving his hand to stop him. He walked up to Marcus. "Being outside exposed to the sun has hastened the dissolution of his body."

"He was beautiful," Marcus said. "Now everything about him is disgusting. My baby brother has turned into a monster. I will never get rid of this sight in my head. Never." He turned away to vomit again. When he recovered, he pointed to the bloody depression in Lucas' head. "Who would do this?"

Argolicus remembered Maria's warning. He wondered what she had meant about lying. And who were *they*? Did she mean the father and the brothers? If so, Marcus might be feigning. The decomposing body was repulsive. Even if Marcus had killed his brother, the sight of the body days later was enough to disturb anyone. And, if Marcus were the killer, then the decomposition could prompt not just revulsion but guilt.

"We could speculate, but that is all it would be," Argolicus said. "Now is the time to take care of Lucas. Get him home or to the clerics to prepare his body for burial."

Marcus nodded and made the sign of the cross three times. "You are right. The sooner he is in the ground, the sooner this ghastly vision will be gone."

Argolicus probed. "Can you think of who would want to do this?"

"My brother," Marcus said. "Father is angry at him, as you saw, but he... he wouldn't do that to anyone. He is strict and blunt but not vengeful. In his own way, he cared about Lucas. Lucas was going off with no prospects. He wanted to support some crazy monk. He didn't want to become a cleric. He was looking at a life of poverty, at least the way he described it."

"And that's why your father is angry? Lucas chose a life outside the family tradition? A life that didn't bring honor to the family?"

"Yes. We would never see him again. Our family would be torn apart. Father believes we each have a responsibility to the family. Father wants the best for all of us."

"By best, you mean wealth and power?"

Marcus thought for a moment. "I hadn't looked at it that way... yes, wealth and power. Status. We live comfortably. Giving up everything makes little sense. Lucas had so much to gain by staying with the family. It doesn't make sense to me and it certainly doesn't to Father."

"But from what I understand, Lucas was already at odds with your father. He had left to travel to Rome. It was happenstance, or fate, or the hand of God, as your father would call it, that he found this monk. Hadn't he already broken with your family?"

Marcus glanced at his brother's body, sprawled and rotting on the ground. "Yes. But we thought he would make a place for himself in the city. As the youngest son, he could gain influence for himself in some political role. Not everyone who meets a monk decides to follow his path."

"Just so," Argolicus said, thinking of Bartholomaeus' reason for cutting off his childhood friendship. He looked at Wiliarit standing among the flowers. His uncle gave him a knowing smile and nodded. "But, the monk is far away. Lucas was killed here. I don't see a connection."

Marcus shook his head, blinked his eyes, and stared again at his brother's body. "I hate to think this was purposeful. I mean against Lucas. I can't think of a reason for anyone to do this. Father and Lucas disagreed about almost everything. Mattheus took Father's side. His return home wasn't pleasant. But killing? Absolutely not. It must have been robbers who were angry he had nothing to steal. It doesn't make sense. To think someone deliberately killed Lucas... because he was Lucas, just doesn't make sense."

He shook his head again and motioned to the slaves. They brought a large blanket and spread it out next to Lucas' body. Four slaves gathered around the body and reached down to lift the body onto the blanket. Marcus counted down one, two, three. At the count of three, the slaves slid their hands under the body and began to lift it. The head wobbled backward and reddish fluid oozed out of the mouth and nose. One slave jumped back, almost losing hold of the body. Marcus signaled another slave to hold the head. The men lifted in unison and brought the body up off the ground. The right arm of the corpse flopped down. A slave reached out to place the arm on the torso. The skin on the hand slid down over the fingers.

Marcus cried out, once again.

Argolicus wondered what the brother knew and whether he had killed Lucas. Whatever the reason, the killing was senseless.

Once the body was on the blanket, the slaves carried it off to the cart and covered it with another cloth. Marcus strode toward his horse nibbling on the fresh grass. But then, he turned around and came back to Argolicus who was helping Wiliarit fill the box of painting supplies.

"You were right to tell us. My father is abrupt and dogmatic. You always made Lucas enthusiastic when you two were young. I liked you for that."

"Lucas was my friend," Argolicus said as Marcus went to his horse, mounted, and followed the cart out of the meadow. He watched the horse thread its way from the meadow.

"Well," Wiliarit said, laying his vellum sheets in the box and closing the lid. "I see his father's imprint."

Argolicus watched his uncle lift the leather strap of the box to his shoulder. "Yes, of course. But he seemed genuinely distressed when he saw the body. He seems just as bewildered as we are." He searched in his folds for the scrap Maria had given him.

"What is it?" Nikolaos asked.

"The sister. She said they were lying. I have it here some-where." He fumbled through his tunic. "Aha," he said, pulling out the folded scrap. He read aloud from the note, 'I will tell you the story of my brother. I will find you.'"

"That doesn't tell us much," Nikolaos said, shaking his head.

"You are best out of it. Stay away from that family. It will only open old wounds," Wiliarit said. He adjusted the strap of his painting box on his shoulder. "Let's go home. I, for one, could use some food." He patted his belly.

"He was my friend," Argolicus said as they all crossed the meadow to head toward the villa. The difference between his laughing, playful friend and the rotten corpse struck him. The gap of years was a blank. He knew little about Lucas. He thought about how he had changed in those years. His vision of himself at fifteen had been to follow in his father's footsteps, grow into the estate, manage the property, and live comfortably. He hadn't envisioned years in Rome and the hard reality of the politics of powerful men.

"You haven't seen him for many years. Getting involved with that family was trouble then. It will be trouble now."

"These theological arguments, especially hating someone for their belief, or even their perceived belief from a narrow mind, make me angry. It's everywhere. People have arguments in the street in Rome. Men get into fights. It makes no sense. Where is the compassion?"

Wiliarit laid a hand on Argolicus shoulder. "You had two losses in quick succession. First, your father and, just when you needed friendship and kindness, you lost your friend. Those are wounds that leave scars."

"Do you think I am taking this too personally... mixing theological debates with my personal loss?"

"Only you can know. But, you could think about your personal involvement. This differs from being the supreme magistrate in Rome and resolving someone else's dilemma. Your memories and personal attachment, including how you feel about that family, may color your thinking."

"You are right. I'm best out of this. We've recognized his body, and the family has Lucas' body. There's no reason to be involved anymore." He smiled at Wiliarit. "I'll think about what you said. It's strange. You arrive and once again I'm mixed up with that family. Let's go home and let it rest." He turned to Nikolaos. "You'd think I'd remember all the old trails, but not just yet. Lead on."

Nikolaos led the way through the thick forest of trees. There wasn't a marked path, but he seemed to know the way. The warmth faded as they threaded through the trees. Argolicus followed, his mind lost in thoughts of his father, his friendship with Lucas, and the abrupt break that had shattered his youth. How had Lucas changed? He knew nothing about him as an adult. Wiliarit was probably right. He remembered a friend from childhood. Adult filters colored his memories. His recent life in Rome. filled with politics and a different corruption than an untended body, colored his memories.

"It's political," Wiliarit said. "It's the same in Constantinople. Theological differences and the Green and Blue Factions, fill the city with disagreements. I thought, at least here, I'd get away from all that and paint in peace."

"No," Argolicus said. "It's everywhere. The governor here spreads corruption and venal grasping rather than a steady hand on his reign. And, here, the Church dominates and controls wealth and the landowners compete with the Church for power."

Wiliarit snorted. "The Church. But our Church came before. The Synod at Chalcedon was a political ploy orchestrated by the Emperor Constantine, not the bishops. Now here we are two centuries later where politics and religion walk hand in hand."

"In Rome, they say Ravenna is the most tolerant city in Italy. Theoderic has proclaimed religious tolerance and keeps those disturbances to a minimum."

"We're a long way from Ravenna. Your friend there, Cassiodorus, does he tell you this is true?"

"He does, in his roundabout way."

"As I said, we're a long way from Ravenna."

"Yes, here tolerance is not a driving force. What makes trade go and who has more slaves these are the matters of concern. It's what people talk about. Look at Lucas' family. They're rich and intolerant."

"As in most places. I need to go to Ravenna and see for myself. I find it hard to believe one city would be so open to tolerance."

The trail opened to fields and they could see the villa and smoke coming from the kitchen chimney.

"Ah, food," Wiliarit exclaimed, smiling. "We're home." He picked up his pace and passed Nikolaos. The equipment in his paint box clacked against the wooden sides.

Three days later, Wiliarit labored at painting in Argolicus' study surrounded by his art supplies. He laid out a large sheet of vellum on an easel and drew the first lines of an illustration based on his sketches from his walks with Nikolaos. Even though the morning air was chilly, the door was open to let in more light.

Cries and clanking sounds rang from the far court where Argolicus and Nikolaos were at their daily fighting practices.

A shadow crossed Wiliarit's work at the same time he heard a female voice cry. "Oh!"

He turned to see a young woman covered in a red cloak.

"I... I thought," she stammered. "Where is Argolicus?"

"You're not mistaken. This is his study. I'm his uncle, Wiliarit, here on a visit. I'm afraid I've taken over his study."

"Wiliarit!" she exclaimed. "I've heard so much about you." Her forehead crinkled in perplexion as if he didn't fit her image. In her early twenties, she had an air of innocence like someone ten years younger.

"You have me at a disadvantage."

"I'm sorry, I was expecting Argolicus. I'm Maria. The sister of Lucas, the man he found in the meadow."

"Maria! I'm delighted. I'm so sorry about your brother. Let me take you to Argolicus, although you could easily find him with all that clanging and shouting." He rose from his seat and joined her at the doorway. His plain monkish robe contrasted with her colorful red cloak as they headed toward the cries and clunks.

Maria smiled. "The action was what Lucas loved. Those two were always doing something active as boys. Lucas used to tell me the wildest stories about shooting arrows from tree branches..."

Wiliarit launched one of his deep belly laughs. "Ah, the arrows. Did he tell you about wounding Julia's pet rabbit?"

"That, too. Argolicus brought out Lucas' adventuresome side." Maria's face changed, her brow wrinkling. "So sad about Julia."

"Ah, yes. Very sad." Wiliarit crossed himself. "Losing a wife and a son. I'm not sure he will replace her. Ah, here we are. The valiant swordsmen."

Argolicus raised his hand to Nikolaos to end their sparring.

Maria turned to Wiliarit. "Thank you. You are nothing like my father..." She paused. "You are nothing like I had imagined." She smiled at him and turned toward Argolicus.

"Maria," Argolicus said, putting down his sword. "Your note was mysterious. Are you here with answers?"

Wiliarit said, "I'm back to painting. Maria, it was a pleasure."

Maria smiled at him and turned to Argolicus. "It's not mysterious. My family..." She groped for words, looking down and then back up to Argolicus. "Lucas took what was his and caused a stir."

Argolicus raised an eyebrow. "What was his? That makes no sense. You need to start at the beginning for me to understand."

"I'm telling you this because Lucas trusted you. Because he trusted you, I trust you. But you must swear you won't tell anyone."

"No one. I'll keep your secret. But why tell me?"

"Because you are the only one who can help. Father and my brothers are angry. They feel the sooner Lucas is buried and forgotten, they can forget the whole thing."

"The whole thing?"

"I'm sorry. I'm not being clear. You are right. I'll start at the beginning."

"Good," Argolicus said as he dipped a cloth into a cistern and wiped his face.

"When each of us was born, Father commissioned an icon to celebrate the birth. He used the Greek iconographer in Rome, Calix. Did you hear of him when you were in Rome?"

Argolicus shook his head. "No. I thought iconographers do not sign their works."

"Yes, that's true," Maria said. "But he is known by word of mouth through his patrons. They are wealthy men like Father and church dignitaries. Anyway, Lucas' icon is lovely, with a worked gilt background. Of course, it is the doctor and evangelist, Luke, his namesake. It is detailed with a winged ox, angels, and the dove descending from heaven."

"Oh, I'm sure Wiliarit would love to see it."

Maria smiled. "Wiliarit... he was painting when I discovered him in your study."

"Yes, but he creates books, not icons."

"When we completed our formation and became members of the Church, Father had stands made for the icons. Not plain wood, but covered in gold leaf and inset with gems. Lucas took his."

"And that's what created the stir? Wouldn't he have a right to take his own icon?"

"That's where it gets complicated, and it involves other people."

"What other people?"

"The bishop."

They stood silently by the cistern. Argolicus felt the sun warm him through his thin exercise tunic. The bishop was a powerful man. He began to understand the complexity.

"The bishop kept the icons for safekeeping."

"Yes, that's it exactly. When Lucas came back from Rome, he wanted the icon. He wanted to give it to that holy man he met, Benedictus. I'm not clear if he wanted to give it to Benedictus or sell it and give the proceeds to Benedictus. Lucas told us he would live with Benedictus. That, alone, was enough to make Father angry. But, the bishop was angry when he took the icon and the stand."

"The bishop was angry at Lucas, and your father was angry at him?"

Argolicus frowned. Lucas was straightforward and outspoken

in his plain-speaking way. He understood how taking a family treasure, even though it theoretically belonged to him, would feel like a betrayal to a man like Bartholomaeus, headstrong and fervent in his religion.

"I'm not sure what happened because I learned most through Father's mutterings and rants. Lucas had left for the north. Father and Bishop Braga argued. Father believed he supported the bishop. The bishop felt the 'safeguarded' treasures were there for the Church. It boiled down to possession and power. Those are two areas where Father should not be crossed."

"And religion," Argolicus could not help saying as he remembered the childhood separation from his friend and his recent encounter with Bartholomaeus.

"Yes, religion. You certainly felt that hard edge. And that is why I am here."

"Why? I don't understand."

"Because someone killed my brother. I want to know who. Father feels Lucas betrayed the family by going outside religious tradition. That meant he went against Father's wishes. He's not a man of forgiveness. I don't want to think a family member killed him."

She paused, staring into the distance where the morning sun shone on the barn and the fields and rough hills beyond.

Argolicus didn't like Bartholomaeus or Maria's arrogant brothers. He felt his old friendship with Lucas welling inside with warm memories. He understood Lucas' desire to get away but didn't understand his new piety brought on by a visit to a hermit.

"Maria, I don't know how I can help you. I can't talk to your father or your brothers. They won't speak to me. I've always had warm feelings for Lucas, but I don't understand his recent turn to piety. Who is this Benedictus?"

"As much as I can tell from what Lucas said, he's a man against the false piety of the Church. I heard he even insulted a group of nearby monks who were supporting him. He believes in simple living and prayer. That's why I'm sure that Lucas was going to sell the icon in Rome and use the money to support his life with Benedictus. That's all I know."

"Whatever the reasons, Lucas decided to leave. I still can't help you. The other place to look would be the church and Bishop Braga, but I would be about as welcome there as at your father's. He would not welcome any questions from me about his feud with your father or what happened to the icon."

Maria sighed. Then she turned, put her arms around Argolicus, and hugged him. "Thank you for listening. I didn't know where to turn."

Then she pulled back and cried. "Lucas, Lucas," she murmured, "what were you thinking? Who did this to you?"

After she headed away on the path toward her home, Argolicus stood in the sunlight, frustrated that he couldn't help. He wanted to know the answer to his friend's murder.

***

"And then she left." Argolicus sat in the courtyard garden with Nikolaos and Wiliarit. They were gathered around a breakfast table with bread, soft cheese, cooked eggs, and olives. Birds sang in the trees. The fountain his mother loved splashed in a soothing rhythm. He picked up his cup of honeyed milk.

"That poor girl," Nikolaos said, shaking his head. "She must look forward to her marriage."

"I'm sure she does," Argolicus said. "What a mixture of sorrow and freedom for a youngster. She was fond of Lucas."

Wiliarit broke off a big piece of bread from the round loaf, dipped it in wine, and chewed. Then he spoke. "I know how we can visit the bishop. I don't know how we can bring any conversation around to Lucas, but I know how to see the bishop."

"How?" Argolicus and Nikolaos asked in unison.

"Pride and greed, They are great motivators." He leaned forward and pulled off another hunk of bread.

"Uncle, don't keep us in suspense. What's your idea?"

"The patroness, Anica Juliana, will have her copy of Dioscorides soon. I'm here to finish up the last illustrations. Then I will look for a new project and a new patron. Surely a provincial bishop tucked away in a small town far away from emperors and princesses would want the services of a scribe with such well-known patrons... yes?"

"You would go to him and ask?"

"Well, he probably can't afford me, but I could arrange a time to speak with him. Religious differences like the nature of Christ are set aside when beautiful possessions enter the picture. I've seen it in Constantinople and Rome. I'm certain the same principles apply in Bruttia. Of course, you would accompany me as a local noble." He leaned back, chewing on the wine-soaked bread, then plopped two olives into his mouth.

Argolicus slapped his hand on the table. "Now that's what I call a good idea."

Wiliarit picked up an egg and tapped the shell with his knife. "We would want a learned, articulate, and observant messenger to deliver my request," he said, looking at Nikolaos.

Nikolaos was up from the table. He ran to the study and returned with a sheet of vellum, a pen, and a pot of ink.

Wiliarit bit into the peeled, hard-cooked egg, causing half to disappear. "Most esteemed excellency, Your Grace, Braga, Bishop of Squillace," he began dictating. "Well, even if it's here in the hills and not the town of Squillace itself, he will eat it up."

Soon he finished the letter, and Nikolaos was off to the bishop's palatial estate on the hill above the meadows.

"Naturally, I will ask to see his treasures so I can 'get a feeling for his excellent taste.' How else could I make a suggestion for the most appropriate book for his collection? Do you think he reads?" He helped himself to a second egg.

"I have no idea. Many clerics don't. He could be the exception, But it doesn't matter. A beautiful book is a symbol of wealth." Argolicus answered. "Do I understand your plan? You will turn your conversation among the bishop's treasures to icons?"

"Aha, you understand," Wiliarit said, chuckling, as he broke off another piece of bread.

"Well, at least we will get his version of what happened with the icon and probably a few choice words about headstrong, misguided men like Lucas. I'm not convinced that will help us find the murderer, but it will shed light on a part of the story we don't know."

Argolicus decided an egg was a good choice. He was hungry after his morning bout with Nikolaos. He reached for the bowl of eggs and said, "Uncle, I don't know what I would have done without you. You are a family treasure."

STRATEGY WITHOUT A PLAN

"I can't stop thinking how lonely Lucas must have been," Argolicus said.

In the study, Argolicus reviewed what had happened in the last few days. Even though Bartholomaeus had separated him from his friend, he should have kept track. He had learned that friends in life were rare. Why hadn't he paid more attention to Lucas? And when Lucas left home and went to Rome, somehow, he should have known and renewed their friendship. He had been in Rome. How had their disconnection remained so strong? How much of it was due to his neglect?

Wiliarit sat dabbing with his paints at a rendering of a bramble. Nikolaos read Herodotus, getting ready for the next oral reading this evening.

"Lonely and disturbed," Wiliarit said, not looking up from his twining bramble, his brush dabbing a dark green at emerging leaves.

"Yes, I feel that somehow I should have..."

"No," Wiliarit said. "Everyone knew you were in Rome. He could just as easily have reached out to you. He didn't. None of this is your fault." He dipped his brush in a cup of water, wiped it clean with a cloth, and laid it down on the table. "Better to concentrate on helping Maria if you want to be soft on someone. There's no going back to change actions. Who do you think killed that lonely, disgruntled man?"

"From what I understand, he didn't feel disgruntled. He was on a path of truth. His truth, but a truth. It's that truth of his that made others disgruntled."

Nikolaos put down the history book. "I hear about that Benedictus. Slaves talk about him. There are rumors. The strongest one is that he insulted a group of monks who reached out to him. I'm not sure about the details. You know how rumors are."

Argolicus nodded. He knew about the distortions of rumors.

"This Benedictus must be an Italian rumor because I haven't heard a word about him in Constantinople," Wiliarit said. "But the western Church and the Eastern Church are at odds, so rumors may not transfer."

Argolicus nodded. "Ah, the Emperor Zeno stirred up a hornet's nest. I think the Acacian division may be with us for a while. Clerics are so touchy about these theological points."

"Precisely," Wiliarit said. "So the ultra-conservative Bishop Braga would staunchly oppose anything that went against his Church, especially some discontented man like Lucas who came with messages counter to tradition. I can tell you right now he would not approve of the Henotikon or any attempts to include 'heretics' in the Church. Of course, that includes us. Our tradition is older than his, but his is the prevailing one here in southern Italy."

"Greed was the main reason he saw us today. You were so right to play to his vanity, Uncle. If we discover who killed Lucas, the family may have to plead to our governor, Venantius. He is just as prideful and greedy. Depending on who killed Lucas, the final decision may come down to who pays the governor the greater fee."

"But, that's the question," Nikolaos said. "Who killed Lucas? Maybe it wasn't about his errant belief but for some other reason."

Argolicus reached behind Wiliarit and pulled a vellum sheet from a stack. "Who do we know so far that had a reason?"

"The father," Nikolaos said. "What an angry man."

Argolicus wrote Bartholomaeus at the top of the sheet. "Yes, his son had disobeyed him. But, what reason would he have to kill him? He is powerful enough to deliver that blow." He scribbled some notes next to the father's name. "But his brother Mattheus is just as strong." He wrote Mattheus. "And he's more irrational than Bartholomaeus. The father has an iron will, but Mattheus seems to fly off the handle, mainly to impress his father. What a tortured father and son relationship."

"Haven't you found that it's often the quiet ones?" Wiliarit said. "What about the brother Marcus? He was the most conciliatory when we announced finding Lucas. After all, he came to retrieve the body while the father stewed in anger. But that could be a show. Maybe he made that show to cover up his guilt."

Argolicus wrote Marcus. "Perhaps. But, he seems easily swayed without conviction. I don't see him getting angry enough, but you are right. It is often the quiet ones."

They sat in silence for a moment, each trying to decipher who would kill Lucas. Then Argolicus picked up his pen and wrote Braga.

"The bishop had motive," he said. "I don't see him physically confronting Lucas. But he has numerous slaves. I'm sure he has a coterie of thugs for enforcement. He has to manage those hundreds of slaves. And from what I gathered from our visit to the bishop, he wields power with the nobles as well. He could have set one or more out to follow and waylay Lucas after he left the palace."

"One supposed heretic?" Nikolaos said. "That doesn't seem worth the risk for a man with so much power. Why would he risk his reputation and all of his worldly goods for one recreant? Lucas didn't have any political power, like his father. Essentially he had been thrown out of the family."

"Nikolaos, you've seen the street brawls in Rome over religious fervor. It doesn't take much to get someone fired up," Argolicus said. "But you are right. The bishop would have little motive to kill a recreant. It would be better to let him leave and never return."

"Yes, Master, but those rioters are street people. I don't see the bishop risking his reputation and position for one person who will soon be gone.",

"Maybe he was in collusion with Bartholomaeus. The bishop

had the thugs at hand. Bartholomaeus needed men for hire. I'm considering possibilities." He scribbled on the vellum sheet.

"Are you forgetting, Maria?" Wiliarit asked. "Talk about quiet ones."

"I understand your 'quiet ones,' but I don't see her instigating murder. I mean, why? She's the one that risked coming here to ask us for help."

They all sat in silence again. Argolicus stared at the vellum sheet, hoping some new thought would come.

Hoofbeats clattered in the courtyard. In minutes, Argolicus' friend, Ebrimuth, found his way to the study door. Every inch of his tall frame declared his heritage from The People—broad shoulders, thick light-blond hair flowed down his back, a dagger strapped to his side over a richly embroidered tunic.

"I knew I'd find you here."

"Ebrimuth, you remember my uncle, Wiliarit."

"The Father and the Son," Ebrimuth said, filling the doorway with his energetic frame.

"Worship and glorify," answered Wiliarit.

"I think we've gathered The People of this area in one place," Argolicus said, laughing.

"Oh, no," Ebrimuth answered. "I have a household full of Our People. Hasn't your mother told you?" He gave Argolicus an arch look with his light blue eyes.

"My mother may hear things, but we don't gossip," Argolicus said.

"Well, I'm here with gossip... news," Ebrimuth said, shoving his broad shoulders through the door as Nikolaos pulled up a chair for him to sit.

"And...?" Argolicus said, smiling. Somehow Ebrimuth and his boundless energy always made him feel invigorated as if the energy transferred from one body to another.

"Your friend Lucas. Everyone is speculating on what could have happened."

"That's what we were doing," Argolicus said, holding up the vellum sheet. "Do you have any thoughts?"

"I do," Ebrimuth said, settling his vibrant body into the chair. "And I don't. Everyone was wondering where Lucas stayed when he was here. He obviously couldn't stay with his family. He came to me."

Argolicus felt the sting of not helping again. "What? With you?"

"He didn't want to cause problems for you. He knew how much his father disliked you... us... Our People. He wanted to retrieve his icon and then go back to Rome. His father told him to never set foot in the house. He was here only a few days. No one would think of looking for him at my house."

"Well, you are right about that," Argolicus said. "It didn't occur to me. I thought he was staying at an inn."

"He wanted safety and a place to be inconspicuous. He felt an inn was too public."

"It worked. No one knew where he was. But what did you think when he disappeared?" Argolicus asked.

Ebrimuth shifted his large shoulders and shook his head of long blonde hair. "I didn't think much except I thought it was strange he hadn't said farewell. He left in the morning for the bishop's palace, and I never saw him again. He didn't say much while he stayed. A bit about his father and his brothers turning against him. It seemed to strengthen his resolve to leave for good. I should have come to you when I noticed he left his travel bag."

"He left for the bishop's palace to get the icon?"

"Yes."

"We visited the bishop. Lucas left with the icon. Not on good terms, but he left. That seems to be the last time anyone saw him. What was in the travel bag?"

"I brought it with me," Ebrimuth said. He pulled a leather strap on his shoulder and removed the satchel. He opened it up and looked at Argolicus. "He's dead now. It won't matter if we look." He pulled his chair closer to the table, upended the bag, and emptied the contents onto the table.

Wiliarit and Nikolaos drew up to the table as Ebrimuth's large hand spread out the contents. Leggings, underwear, two tunics. A book. Nothing.

"No papers. Nothing that helps us find a murderer," Argolicus said as the others pulled back. "Are you sure he said nothing that might help?"

"He wasn't chatty. Twice he said, 'I'm done with Bruttium.' That's it."

Argolicus picked up the vellum sheet and stared. "His father out of pride. His older brother. The bishop."

"Maybe it was a robbery gone wrong," Nikolaos said. "He was fighting for his life, and a robber hit him."

"Maybe. But look at those clothes. Was he dressed more formally when he left for the bishop's palace? Did he look rich?" Argolicus said.

"No," Ebrimuth said. "His clothing was indistinguishable from what you see there."

"I'm missing something. Something important. I feel like it's right in front of me, but I'm not seeing it." Argolicus slapped down the vellum sheet.

"I could get one of my men to ask around. See if there's any news about somebody suddenly rich or who left. Nikolaos could do the same thing. Ask questions where we would get no answers."

"I could do that," Nikolaos said. "It's worked in the past."

Ebrimuth started putting the clothing back in the satchel. "This belongs to his family now. Do you think they want it?"

"Unlikely," Argolicus said. "But that reminds me. I need to send a note to Maria. Just a quick one telling her I've found nothing. We could give the contents to her. She may want to give these things to a slave."

"I'm off then," Ebrimuth said. He stood up, patted Argolicus on the shoulder, and strode out the door.

"Such energy," Wiliarit said, nodding toward the empty doorway.

Argolicus smiled. "He's a doer, not a thinker. He must have been uncomfortable with Lucas brooding. Such opposites. But then Lucas found a solution to his problem. Hidden in plain sight." He turned to Nikolaos. "I'll write a note to Maria. You can take it and this satchel. Then spend some time with servants and slaves. See if you can learn anything."

Argolicus scribbled on another sheet of vellum, folded it, and handed it to Nikolaos.

Wiliarit stirred a pot of paint and dipped in a brush. "I'm thinking about the Church. Braga is more than one man insatiable for ownership. He is the Church."

Outside, a new set of hooves clattered in the courtyard. Argolicus stood. "It seems to be a day for visitors."

A young slave girl knocked at the entrance to the study. "Your mother wants you in the *atrium*."

MATTHEUS AT THE DOOR

The elder brother Mattheus' embroidered shoes slapped the marble floor as he paced. He stopped when Argolicus entered the *atrium*, balancing his bulk with widespread feet.

"I'll leave you to talk," Amalina, Argolicus' mother, said. Her light blue tunic reflected the light in her eyes. Her long braid swished against her back, and the dagger scabbard hanging from her waist shifted against her thigh as she walked toward the kitchen.

"Mattheus," Argolicus said. "Welcome. Have you found out something about Lucas?"

Mattheus ignored his question. "I thought my father was clear. Stay out of our family business. We already asked you, and the next thing I hear, you've been visiting the bishop, asking questions." He brought his bulky frame up close to Argolicus. "Stay away."

Argolicus kept his anger in check and expressed his first thought. "Is this you speaking your father's words?"

"It doesn't matter who says the words. They are clear enough. Stay away." Mattheus crossed his arms over his silk tunic.

Argolicus kept silent, looking the posturing man in the eye.

"Yes, my father sent me," Mattheus finally continued. He dropped his arms and balled his fists. "He can't stand the thought of you. This is a family matter. You are no part of our family. Stay away. Don't get involved."

Argolicus thought about telling him about the nature of the visit, Wiliarit and the book, but he knew it would be useless. And, in a sense, he was right. And, if word had come to Bartholomaeus, then something was off because the visit was about creating a book. They had created a reason to visit the bishop, but it was all the bishop knew. He hedged.

"I can't feed your fears. The visit was about another matter, not Lucas. If I see the bishop, or the wine merchant, or the horse breeder, that is my concern." He was finding his anger was pushing at him. He could feel his face getting red.

"But my father heard..." Mattheus spluttered and then grew silent.

"Rumors are not truth. You stay out of my matters. I'll stay out of yours. Tell your father that is my agreement."

Mattheus lost his bluster. "I will." He turned and shuffled across the marble, his silks rustling in empty bravado. Then he stopped and turned. "Why? Why do you care about Lucas' murder?"

"He was my friend. I cared about him. I'm baffled why he didn't get in touch with me if he was having serious trouble."

"He wasn't having 'serious trouble' that I know. Of course, Father was angry at him and his crazy plan to go follow a monk in a cave. If you were a father, wouldn't that give you concern?"

Argolicus hadn't seen it that way before. His own prejudice and lingering resentment stood in his way. He considered the new perspective. "I was thinking of Lucas' right to make his own decisions. You are right. I would have questions about the wisdom of such a major decision."

"He was my brother. I thought he was doing it out of spite. I can't imagine a rational man giving up everything. His status. It was the rest of his life." Mattheus pulled his forehead together in a frown. "It's unthinkable."

"Religious callings puzzle those who don't experience them," Argolicus said. "I don't understand, and, yet, my uncle, was called to be a monk. It doesn't make him less of a person. Just different. He is quite pleasant company."

"Yes, but he's not part of the Church. That's why Father

wanted Lucas away from him long ago. Do you think Lucas was rebelling against…"

"No, I don't think that. Lucas was wiser than to bear out a grudge against your father for something that happened long ago. If he was following a monk, it was because that monk spoke to him, not because your father forbade meeting with Wiliarit years ago. Our Church. The King, Theoderic, and all of us of the People follow a Christian tradition that is older than your present Trinitarian theology. Lucas wasn't a student of theology. That is different from a man of faith."

"I'm not prepared to discuss theology. Think of me as a man of faith, one different from yours. I came to deliver my father's message." Mattheus started to turn and then said, "I remember how Lucas enjoyed your company. You two had fun, from what I can tell. I'm not sure I ever had fun."

He startled Argolicus. "You didn't play as a child?"

"A different kind of play—board games, puzzles. But I didn't have a friend to romp through the woods, climb trees. I didn't have adventures like the two of you. As the eldest, Father expected me to set an example for the others. My example was the Church. My example *is* the Church. I think Lucas was impetuous and foolish to leave our family." Mattheus crossed his arms over his chest and dipped his chin.

"With his new turn, I'm not certain he would consider me his friend." Argolicus tried to imagine giving up his life to live in a cave. He couldn't. "But, regarding your father, I see no reason for us to cross paths."

Mattheus lifted his hands in a placating gesture, turned, and left the *atrium.*

Argolicus walked the passage to the *peristylum,* lost in thought. Lucas hadn't come to see him on his return. From a rational point of view, he could understand how he didn't want to stir up old troubles with his father. But even after he'd had a row with his father, he went to Ebrimuth. Not a word to his old friend. Not even a note. He felt slighted.

Was he good at friendship? He'd known Ebrimuth since childhood and would trust his life with his wild friend. But, all the time he'd been in Rome and known people, even worked at meeting people, he'd not had a friend. Not someone he could spend time with in a casual way or share his thoughts. Maybe that was why he was so upset with Lucas' murder. He stopped pacing and sat down on a bench in front of the fountain.

He was taking this murder personally. With all the crimes and murders he had investigated in Rome, it was a matter of getting to the root of the problem. This time he felt the loss. He thought about all the family members and friends he'd spoken with who had been feeling loss and bewilderment.

"There you are," Wiliarit said, approaching from the kitchen with a bowl of radishes. "Want a radish? I think this is the best time of year for radishes, juicy and tart." He held out the bowl.

Argolicus took a large, red radish, trimmed and scrubbed clean, and bit in. He watched the fountain water play in the light of the open room.

"Lost in thought?" Wiliarit asked as he sat on the bench beside Argolicus.

"Mmmm," Argolicus mumbled, chewing.

"The brother. What did he want?"

"He was his father's messenger. Stay out of our family affairs. Somehow they knew we'd been to visit the bishop. News travels quickly. Of course, I couldn't tell him his own sister had asked us to look into Lucas' death. But that wasn't what I was thinking about."

"What, then?"

"Friendship. How precious it is. Especially for me. I don't have many friends. Knowing many people and having friends are two different things. Even though I hadn't seen Lucas in years, his death touched me. I thought I was inured to death and murder, but when it happens to a friend, I can't help but feel a loss."

Wiliarit stared at the one large radish left in the bowl. "You feel a personal responsibility to find the killer. Not just because Maria asked for help."

"Yes. I can't seem to separate her request from my personal interest. And… I'm angry. Angry at Lucas for not reaching out to me."

"That's the hard part, not being able to control other people's actions. I have my faith when I am disappointed. What do you have?" Wiliarit took the last radish, popped it in his mouth, and crunched in satisfaction.

"That's just it. I think of myself as rational, especially when investigating a murder. But feelings keep creeping in. I feel slighted because Lucas didn't contact me. He stayed with Ebrimuth and never said a word to me. I have sympathy for Maria. Not just that her brother was murdered, but that Bartholomaeus is so overbearing. And, then, how can I help her if I'm not rational?"

"Here's what I've learned if you don't mind advice from an old man."

"No, no. Tell me."

"When emotions start to knock you off-kilter, keep doing what you are doing. Just the physical activity helps to put everything back in perspective."

Argolicus nodded.

"And, find a wife. A good woman helps keep you balanced."

Argolicus chortled. "Now you sound like Mother."

"Are you talking about me?" Amalina entered the *peristylum* from the direction of the kitchen. She crossed the marble floor with a grace most middle-aged women had lost years before.

"Mother, you'll be happy to hear that Uncle Wiliarit has suggested I find a wife."

She raised an eyebrow at Wiliarit.

"Amalina, you know how we all respect your wisdom."

"I know something is up when my brother tries to flatter me. What are you two plotting?"

"Mother, it's nothing. Uncle was consoling me... in his way. It's just that I'm surprised at how Lucas' murder is affecting me."

"Not by that insufferable man who was just here?"

"No. I think he's even more lost than I am. His father rules his life. I'm not sure he has an original thought or would recognize one if he had it. He's like most bullies. Empty inside. I'm upset about Lucas."

"Lucas was a childhood friend. Of course, it upset you," Amalina said as she wrinkled her brow in sympathy.

"It's not that. I feel as though the friendship didn't mean that much to him. He stayed with Ebrimuth, and I didn't even know he was here."

"Ebrimuth explained why," Wiliarit said. "I think you may be frustrated that you can't find his killer."

"Maybe." Argolicus frowned. Was his mind so untrustworthy? He had been fond of Lucas. They had been best friends when they were young. "Maybe, I'm mourning my youth."

Amalina said, "Maybe, the best act of friendship you can do now is to find his killer."

Argolicus smiled. "Mother, you are always right... except when you talk about marriage."

All three of them laughed.

"That's for another day," Wiliarit said. "Let's get back to thinking about the possible killers. We didn't add bandits or robbers to your list."

"I'm off to talk to the overseer. Hand me that bowl. I'll send it to the kitchen." She turned to look at Argolicus. "You could help me with running the estate. When was the last time you talked with Lucius? No, don't answer. I know it's been a while. You could add that to your schedule along with fighting and reading."

Wiliarit gave her the empty radish bowl. Amalina walked

toward the kitchen, her long, blonde braid swaying down her back. Argolicus mentally added managing the estate, at least talks with Lucius, the overseer, to his daily activities. Then his mind returned to the murder.

"Bandits seem unlikely. Except for the fact that Lucas was alone, he wasn't a likely robbery target. He was wearing a linen tunic, but nothing, except the ring, made him a likely target, and the ring was still on his finger. No, it was someone with a different motive."

"Well, the icon is missing. From what the deacon said, it was in a modest cloth sack—hardly an item to catch a bandit's eye. You're probably right. What about that brother that was just here?"

"If anything, his actions convinced me that he is just a shell. He doesn't have the spirit to kill so brutally. We can't rule him out, but he is empty inside. Conniving, possibly, but brutal, no."

Argolicus watched the sunlight playing in the flow of water in the fountain.

"Master," Nikolaos said, rushing into the open space. "I delivered the note, but there is a complication. Everything is chaotic at Bartholomaeus' house. Maria was in tears. I could hear Bartholomaeus arguing with Mattheus. This murder has caused confusion in that house."

Argolicus looked up. "I just told Mattheus I would stay out of their family's affairs. But we will keep looking for the murderer."

"You will have an uncomfortable conversation, then," Nikolaos said. "Maria is on her way."

"This will be tense," Wiliarit said. "I'm going to find some fortification for us all." He headed toward the kitchen.

THE BISHOP'S COLLECTION

The sun hid behind high clouds the next day as Wiliarit, Argolicus, and Nikolaos rode toward the bishop's palace. The horses pranced in the spring air, ready for a gambol. The men each kept a firm hand on the reins.

"Ah, what a smooth gait. Argolicus, you should ride more. No offense to Nikolaos, but riding will improve your skills just as much as all that pretend fighting you do."

Nikolaos kept silent.

"A new stallion," said Argolicus. "He's particular about who he lets ride without resistance. I'll tell you the story about how we got him later. His name is Mercury's Flame, but we call him Flame."

Wiliarit patted the big red horse on the neck and whispered his name, "Flame." The stallion responded with a nod and a twist of his ears. "And look, all that sunshine yesterday opened more flowers. We're in luck, Nikolaos. I'll finish this book project in no time."

As they approached the palace, Argolicus saw movement everywhere. Slaves hurried around the palace grounds carrying equipment or working on building new structures. Children scurried carrying baskets. Crews of men worked on walls, pathways, and new buildings.

"More people than most towns," Argolicus said as he nodded toward the palace. "This new bishop has been busy while I was away in Rome."

"Aggressively so," Wiliarit said. "It's been longer than that since I looked up that hill."

***

"I was thinking of the letters of the Church Father Ignatius," Wiliarit said to Bishop Braga. "he advised, 'Follow the lead of your bishop.' Does that seem fitting?"

Bishop Braga stood eye to eye with Nikolaos, but their height was the only similarity. Where Nikolaos was lithe, supple, and diminutive, Braga was broad and labored. His snub nose gave his face a child-like quality. He walked stiff-legged, like a dog approaching a fight. He wore his hair slicked with scented pomade above his round, smooth face. Although his clerical garments were plain wool, he wore several jeweled rings besides his bishop's ring. His elaborately worked gold pectoral cross hung on a heavy gold chain. His voice was resonant with rounded vowels that would carry to the back of the nave.

"Would I be the only one to have this text?" the bishop asked.

"The only one in southern Italy," Wiliarit said. "Perhaps if you could show me your collection, I could get a better feel for how to produce the book and the most appropriate text to add to your library."

They were gathered in the *salutorium*, grand presence room, a large, empty, expansive room barren of furniture except for the bishop's ornately carved chair. Three deacons stood in silence behind the bishop dressed in similar clerical dark woolen robes.

Argolicus watched the round bishop puff with pride even though the bishop's words told a different story.

"Well, you must realize," he nodded at Wiliarit, "that this is nothing like you see in Constantinople or Rome." He looked at Argolicus, "Your Excellency, I hope, with friends like Boethius, you will not disparage our humble cumulation, but you will see what we have is quite excellent. The Church cannot survive without support. We are the guardians of local wealth. The wealth supports the Church."

Argolicus realized the bishop knew more about him than they had intended for this visit. He decided to speak as little as possible and let Wiliarit lead while he observed. He knew Nikolaos, silent in this situation, would also watch everything. They could compare insights once they returned home.

Braga led them out of the *salutorium* with his stiff-legged walk into a long hallway where slaves bustled on errands. Outside, they followed a long portico whose arches looked out onto a vast courtyard garden filled with shrubs and herbs. The sun broke through the clouds sending rays streaming light into the garden greenery, shimmering on the leaves. At the end of the covered walkway, they came to a large warehouse with a transverse bar that slid in a groove carved into the floor in front of the door. Braga signaled to the slaves guarding the entrance. They stooped to unlock the pin that held the great locking beam in place and slid the beam along its course groove on the stone floor to bar the door.

"In here," Braga said, "we store goods for safekeeping." He led them into the warehouse filled with boxes of all sizes and floor-to-ceiling shelving where luxury items lay side by side in no seeming order. Gold glittered on uncovered items while several shelves were arrayed with icons of saints with gilt halos, some with entire backgrounds of gold. Another shelf contained goblets of gold and silver, many set with large glittering stones or pearls. In one corner, heaps of swords and daggers leaned against the wall.

Three slave women worked among the treasures, brushing away dust and wiping surfaces with soft cloths. Their chatter ceased as the group entered.

"The Church cannot survive without support. We are the guardians of local wealth. The wealth supports the Church, and the Church supports the land. Mico," he said, turning to a deacon, "Open the treasure room."

The deacon was much taller than the bishop. Underneath his plain robe, his body emanated power in contrast to the bishop's posturing. His dark brown eyes fastened on Wiliarit and, then, Argolicus before he turned to the door. He unclasped a large lock and opened the door into another room.

"We hold our supporters' personal treasures here," Braga said as he led them all into the room. "They add to our resources."

"I'm getting a sense of your preferences," Wiliarit said, gazing around the array, his eyes taking stock of the goods.

The bishop looked up at the large scribe. A flicker of a grimace crossed his face before he composed his expression into a smile. "Oh, no, these are not my personal preferences. These are goods given to the Church for safekeeping. They reflect the tastes of their owners."

Argolicus held his tongue when he heard the word given. Braga had a way of distorting his language to make it appear the goods here were his.

Wiliarit nodded and then asked, "So these beautiful items," he waved his massive arm to encompass everything in the present room and the room they had just left, "are given to the Church. Such a tribute to your spiritual leadership."

"Oh. we do have donations," Braga tried to look humble. "In that room," he said, pointing to the first room, "are goods donated to the Church. Some are bequests of deceased members, and some are given in true generosity by our fold. As I said, without the support of our patrons, the Church would not flourish." His chest expanded, almost reaching the expanse of his middle girth.

"And this room?" Wiliarit questioned. "What about the goods in this room?"

"Well," Braga said with hesitation. "These are here for safekeeping."

"Safekeeping?" Wiliarit echoed Argolicus' thought.

"Yes, safekeeping. In Bruttia, we have so much unrest. At times, the unrest surges into violence. You may not have heard of the local bishop who was murdered several years ago." He glanced at Argolicus. "In the north, the King's peace reigns. Here, far from Ravenna and the heretic king, the people are dissatisfied. Venantius, our governor, is more interested in acquiring wealth than governing. So we must take care of ourselves. Patrons of the Church send us articles, which we may use while they are here, for safekeeping in our secure warehouse. For instance, our closest neighbor and largest patron, Bartholomaeus, has many items here. As a wealthy landowner, he feels vulnerable to the local unrest."

"Yes, I know of him," Wiliarit said. "his son was brutally murdered while out in the countryside. I'm sure you heard about it. I was the one who discovered his body. Gruesome."

"Bartholomaeus was here. He told me about his son's murder. And the discovery." He flashed a look at Argolicus.

Argolicus knew the bishop was well aware of who he was and his religious heritage. The bishop was wily, not saying anything but conveying that he knew at least part of their ruse. But, that would not keep them from exploring what was here at the bishop's palace.

"Ah, Lucas," Braga said. "A young man who strayed from the Church. He was here recently. He's... he was quite the brash man. Imagine! He tried to tell us we, the Church, should let go of material things and lead people in the spirit of Christ."

"In the spirit of Christ?" Wiliarit asked. "Do you mean like Peter?"

"Yes, exactly like Peter in the Acts of the Apostles. To give up everything. We have our Tradition. Tradition keeps the body of the Church together, leading people to participate in sound ways. Without the support of physical goods, the Church would flounder."

Wiliarit nodded.

Bishop Braga continued, "He pestered me with his talk. I gave him to Mico to claim his icon and be gone."

"Yes, Your Grace. He found the icon, wrapped it in cloth, and left." The deacon gestured toward a shelf of icons.

"So, these items in safekeeping belong to their owners, are kept here to be safe, but are accessible at any time to their owners?" Wiliarit asked.

"Exactly," Braga answered. "It's an arrangement for mutual protection. Should either our church buildings here or the landowner's villas come under threat, we support each other with men and arms. I'm sure you saw some of our weapons in the other room."

Wiliarit continued, "So when that young man Lucas came here to retrieve an icon, there was no problem?"

"No, no, no. The goods are here. Mico or another deacon unlocks the warehouse and oversees the removal. We want to make sure no other goods are taken that belong to other patrons."

"Ah," Wiliarit said. "That makes sense."

Argolicus nodded agreement, thinking of the ways avaricious men took any opportunity to gain more, more of anything that would add to their personal riches.

Wiliarit asked, "And the icon was all that Lucas wanted?"

"Your Grace, with your permission," the deacon Mico said. Braga nodded his head. "He, Lucas, the young man... he wanted just the icon. But you have to understand that we were reluctant. Although he was like his father—committed, fevered—for him, everything was black and white. To combat his father's zeal, he found his own. He was against the Church and our traditions. Our Church, the Church that leads the community here. I tried to persuade him to leave the icon here, or at least wait until we consulted with his father, Bartholomaeus. But no, he wanted the icon. He said it was his birthright. He wanted to... it was a garbled story... give it to some man near Rome. Not a priest, not a monk, just a man who lives in a cave. He took it, wrapped it in linen, and placed it in a cloth carrying bag."

"Interesting," Wiliarit said. "In my travels, I've encountered many interpretations of Church and property. This thinking of Lucas harkens back to the beginnings. But the Church has grown since then."

Braga and the deacon, Mico, nodded.

"Indeed," Braga said. "I was glad to see him go. We have enough trouble here with displaced farmers and the like always asking for more. More support. More work. It's impossible to give to everyone. I've talked with Bartholomaeus about this. It's the landowners' place," he glanced at Argolicus again, "to keep the people in check."

Argolicus crossed his arms over his chest, using a physical action to keep himself from speaking. This bishop—young, power-hungry, and determined to remain in charge—did his utmost to keep his wealthy followers under his wing.

Wiliarit interrupted his thoughts.

"But, let's look at some of the items. Your Grace, show me which are your favorites. That will help me determine if Ignatius would be an apt selection for you. You are still interested, yes?"

"Oh, yes," Braga said. "Let me show you some icons. My books are scant."

THE MARIA QUANDARY

"Ah," Wiliarit said as a slave brought a tray with eggs, honey vinegar, pine nut sauce, and a small pitcher of *garum* and laid it out on a table in the *peristylum*. "You see, we can meet here." He took an egg from the bowl, dipped it in the sauce, and poured on a drop of *garum*. "Just what I needed."

A second slave arrived with the paint box and a board.

"I can paint here in the light," Wiliarit said, producing a vellum sheet and attaching it to the board. He settled in on the bench next to Argolicus as the slaves arranged his painting equipment.

Argolicus ignored the food as he listened to Nikolaos reporting on his delivery.

"You could hear Bartholomaeus arguing with Braga, the bishop. Not the words, just the argument. I went in by the slave entrance. A slave took your note to Maria."

"Why was Braga there? It must be important for him to leave his palace and go to Bartholomaeus," Argolicus said.

"I don't know. Their voices were harsh. The father is very loud. As I said, I couldn't hear the words, just the loud voices."

The afternoon sunlight slanted on the water fountain.

"Borage," Wiliarit said. "Just the right herb to add to the sauce. Delightful. Amalina knows how to keep a good kitchen. Try one."

Argolicus took an egg, dipped it in the honeyed sauce, and poured out a drop of *garum*. He bit into the tasty concoction and turned his head as a slave entered the *peristylum* followed by Maria. She entered the sunlight and crossed the marble floor.

"I came as soon as I could," Maria said. "Lucas taught me all the trails and even the ways here that have no trails." She smiled.

"Maria," Wiliarit said. "Sit down, sit down. Have an egg."

Maria came over and sat down next to Argolicus, ignoring the eggs. She threw back the folds of her red cloak. "Ah, the sun. A warm March day. Who could believe all these troubles on such a lovely day? But, I am here about trouble."

She turned to Argolicus, who asked, "There's more trouble? Lucas' death isn't enough?"

"I'm afraid. Father is angry. He seems to be angry at everyone and everything. He had a huge argument with Mattheus when he came back from seeing you. Father hit him. Marcus tried calming him down. He can usually get Father to calm down, but not today. I thought he would hit Marcus, too. But, he retreated just in time. Then Bishop Braga came. I don't know why. Ordinarily, Father goes to the palace. Their shouts echo throughout the house. Father is terrifying when he goes into a rage." She took in a deep breath. Her large eyes widened. "I'm afraid. I don't know what to do."

Argolicus remembered how Bartholomaeus had threatened Lucas and kept him in a room for days. How just when he needed a friend after his father's death, his best friend had been locked away and threatened with beatings. The rage Bartholomaeus had poured out on Wiliarit, who was with his sister in her grief. It had been a defining moment. He had questioned Christianity, and the questions had never left.

Maria interrupted his thoughts. "I want to be somewhere else until the wedding. It's just weeks away. Father has suggested I put it off for a year of mourning. I can't live there. I can't stand it. Living in fear, afraid to say anything about Lucas while my heart is breaking at his death. When Father goes into a rage, it can last for days. I'm terrified he will try to delay the wedding. It's like a dark cloud in our house." She closed her eyes to stop tears, but they rolled down her cheeks.

Nikolaos slipped away into the house.

"And, and," she continued, "thank you for your note. I shouldn't have asked for your help. It complicated everything.

The bishop is angry. My father is angry. Lucas was honest. I'm sorry I preyed on your old friendship. How could one honest man cause so much turmoil? Do you think my father could have done this? Or sent a slave to do it? Should I be afraid of my father? I mean, really afraid?" The tears kept rolling down, and she started sobbing.

Wiliarit sat as if in contemplation, but Argolicus knew his uncle's mind was churning with ideas.

Argolicus said, "Didn't your mother have a sister? Don't you have cousins? Can you stay with them until your father calms down?"

Nikolaos came back into the garden and handed Maria a linen cloth. She took the cloth, wiped her cheeks and sniffling nose, and then shook her head.

"They moved north. That was soon after your father died. There is no one." She subsided into tears again.

Argolicus felt trapped. He wanted to help her but already felt his alliance with this family had caused too much trouble.

They all sat quietly in the March sun, each with their own thoughts.

"I came as soon as I could," Amalina said, rushing out from the kitchen area with a cup in her hand. "Nikolaos told me Maria was here." She sat down on the bench next to Maria and put her arm around the young woman's shoulder. "Here, drink some of this tea."

Maria wiped her face again, looked up, and took the cup. She sipped the cup. And sipped again. "This is good. Thank you."

"Why don't you come inside with me," Amalina said as she took the cup from Maria. "You can drink the tea, and I'll give you a snack. You'll feel better."

Maria nodded. Amalina guided her out of the *peristylum* into the back of the house.

"Well," said Wiliarit, dabbing green onto an outlined leaf on his board. "What a quandary. She comes to the one place that will infuriate her father the most. The two of us being unacceptable heretics." He reached out and patted Argolicus' shoulder.

Argolicus shook his head. "I feel for her, but we can't get involved at that personal level. I told her I would look into Lucas' murder, but then today, I told Mattheus that I would stay out of their family business. I've put myself in a box and don't know how to get out."

He took an egg and dipped it in the sauce. "I think I'm eating more since your arrival." He patted his stomach.

"Food is a solace," Wiliarit said, reaching for another egg. "Especially in worrisome times. Let's see if we can solve the murder and rid you of your burden. What about the other brother, Marcus?" He plopped the rest of the egg in his mouth, wiped his fingers, and began dabbing tiny yellow dots in the center of a white flower.

"Unless he did it at his father's bidding. It's hard to tell," Argolicus answered. "It's hard to tell about any of them. Maybe the father, given to rage, hired thugs."

"None of them look guilty," Wiliarit said, applying yellow dots to another white flower. Nikolaos moved behind him to watch him work.

"You've traveled to cultured places like Constantinople, Burgundia, and even Rome, but in the role of a bookmaker. From a monk's perspective, people reveal their shortcomings in the eyes of God. But, as a magistrate, I've found that people hide their feelings and especially their motivations. The innocent can appear guilty, and the guilty act reverent and beyond reproach."

Wiliarit nodded his head as he concentrated on the center of another flower on the vellum.

"And, how can we really know people?" Argolicus continued. "My feelings for Lucas are based on a boy I knew over fifteen years ago. Who knows how he matured, or even if he matured? Remember how he was a daredevil, hanging from tree branches, and riding horses at full gallop over fields riddled with rodent holes. He took risks without thinking."

Wiliarit nodded again.

"We don't know what he said or did to other people when he came back from the north. He could have angered one of his brothers about something other than going to live with the monk. He could have offended anyone. We don't know who he saw or what he did."

"Those look so lifelike," Nikolaos said, peering over Wiliarit's shoulder.

"Thanks to you for showing me where to find those spring flowers. Do you have any thoughts about Lucas?"

Nikolaos was quiet for a moment. "I agree with Argolicus. We don't know how he acted as an adult. We don't know enough."

Wiliarit went back to the leaves with a different green. "Yes, as a monk, I devote my life to God. I have made my choice. I can understand how Lucas could make a similar decision. My interaction with Bartholomaeus years ago was painful, and from what you say, his temper and strict beliefs have not softened over the years. But, I am also wondering how he could have angered Braga."

"I'm listening," Argolicus said. Bartholomaeus' clash with Wiliarit and the end of his friendship with Lucas was tied in his mind with his father's death.

"Clerics have a different focus than, say, a monk. While I have a personal relationship with God, and a cleric may, too, the cleric has a responsibility to guard and carry on the traditions of the Church. It doesn't matter what branch or belief it is. The cleric's responsibilities are to the Church. Lucas may have said something against the Church."

"Quite likely," Argolicus said, "considering how fervent he was about his new calling."

"Yes, but murder as a response? Lucas was going away, and

from what we know, he was not coming back. That's one reason his father was angry ..."

"It's all settled," Amalina said, coming into the *peristylum* with Maria by her side. Maria was smiling.

"What?" Argolicus asked, jarred out of his thinking.

"Maria will stay here until her wedding. We have plenty of room. It's not a problem. All we have to do ..."

"Mother, we can't. No. I promised Mattheus we'd stay out of their family affairs."

Maria's smile disappeared. Tears glistened at the corners of her eyes.

"No one should live in fear from their own family. You of all people should know injustice takes many forms."

Argolicus knew she was right. Maria needed protection. Why couldn't she find it somewhere else? He felt the box shrink around him. Now, his mother had given her word. For The People, a word given was immutable, the basis of trust. Now he had given his word, and so had his mother. They were at cross purposes.

"I gave my word."

"And so did I," Amalina said.

They stared at each other. Wiliarit and Nikolaos both scrutinized the painting. Maria's eyes began to well over above her trembling lip. The fountain burbled on in the sunlight until Amalina smiled.

"We can both keep our word. I will go with Maria to gather some things and bring them back along with her maid. You will stay here, so you won't be involved."

"But, she will be here, in our house. I am the head of the household. Bartholomaeus will see me as interfering."

"Did you know Lucas was with Ebrimuth?"

"No."

"Then why would anyone need to know she is here?"

Silence in the *peristylum*.

"Good. That's settled then," Amalina said. She smiled and turned to Maria. "We'll have lunch and then go."

Maria smiled in relief and murmured, "Thank you."

Amalina put her arm around Maria's shoulder and turned toward the kitchen.

"Mother," Argolicus said. "We will accompany you to the meadow and wait for you there to escort you back." Although he felt he was not keeping his word in a strict sense, he was relieved that they could keep Maria safe. Bartholomaeus was unpleasant and threatening.

"Lunch is an excellent idea," Wiliarit said. "What a beautiful day to eat here in the sunshine."

The meadow was bright in the afternoon sun with more flowers than just a few days ago when they had found Lucas. Nikolaos brought the entire group through the woods where the trees had leafed out in a green canopy that thinned as they arrived in the meadow.

"I'll have to come back again when I am in search of flowers," Wiliarit said as he pushed wisps of forest undergrowth out of his way on the path. He held tight to the strap of his paintbox. "This place is beautiful. Look how green the trees are. And this meadow. It's like the center of spring. I see how the ancient Romans loved their goddess, Flora."

Maria said, "I love coming here. It's one place I will miss when I am married. This is where you found Lucas?" Her red cloak shone brilliantly in the sun, matching the red meadow flowers.

"Yes," Argolicus, Nikolaos, and Wiliarit said in unison.

Argolicus continued, "It was a gruesome sight. I wouldn't have recognized him except for the ring. You are better off missing that view of your brother."

"I saw him," Maria said. "I watched the slaves clean his body." She was silent for a moment. "But these flowers are like his spirit. That joy of life. That's what I miss. I was worried when he said he wanted to follow a monk, but now that I've spent time with Wiliarit, I see that doesn't mean giving up a joy of life. I can understand him better now." She smiled at Wiliarit.

Wiliarit nodded. "I'll do more sketches while you are all at the villa." He opened his box and pulled out brushes.

"I've been thinking about that," Argolicus said. "Maria, I know you go for walks by yourself, but going to your father's house to retrieve your things... I think you may need protection. Wiliarit can stay here, but I will go up to the house. I won't go inside, but you'll know I am just outside the door."

Amalina said, "Thank you. Your kindness always comes through."

Argolicus never knew what to do when his mother complimented him. "All right, then. Let's head on. Wiliarit, we'll see you soon."

Wiliarit stooped over a tiny red flower. He stood up. "I'll be here." Then he crouched down to get a closer look.

The nearer they came to the villa, the more Argolicus' apprehension grew. Giving Maria safe harbor was right in one way. In another, he was in the midst of doing exactly what he said he would not do, meddle in the family affairs. But his mother had given her word. He refused to disappoint her and her right thinking.

In a few more minutes, they were outside the large villa. Among the busy servants and slaves bustling around the villa walls, a few servants and several elegantly equipped horses clustered toward the side of the imposing main door. The bishop, Argolicus thought. Or some other wealthy noble.

Beyond the villa, the fields bustled with slaves clearing for spring planting. He realized why Nikolaos had been busy in his personal herb garden setting out new plants. Herbs for curing. Herbs for healing.

They gathered at the edge of the woods. All of them looking at the villa walls.

Amalina wrapped her large *palla* around her shoulders, took Maria's hand, and led her to the side work entrance where they disappeared. Argolicus and Nikolaos found a large tree and waited in the shade by the trunk. Nikolaos pulled out a small book. Argolicus groaned inside. Quiet time was always a time for instruction or practice, even in times as tense as this. Argolicus hoped his mother would successfully get Maria out without being spotted. He thought of her as a matron but realized she was brave in her own way, ready to stand up for her beliefs.

Argolicus was about to share his thoughts with Nikolaos to

interrupt any intentions of practicing Greek. But, the eldest brother Mattheus suddenly stood in the main doorway, his face grim above his silks.

"Inside," Mattheus called, waving his arm toward the door. No coming to meet them or polite greeting. "Come inside now. This is the end of your meddling."

Nikolaos put away the book and followed Argolicus into the *atrium* of the big villa. Inside the room with its brightly painted walls and colorful mosaic floor, Amalina looked on stoically as Bartholomaeus gripped Maria's arm. Maria was not in tears even though her cheek had a big red patch. She looked at Argolicus with quiet desperation.

Seeing the red patch on the girl's cheek was all it took for Argolicus to side with his mother. Bartholomaeus was like many men, rough with his family. Maria was in danger from her own father. He'd seen it before. The hitting always got worse, never lessened. He wanted her to stay safe and felt powerless to do anything. He looked at his mother, who wore her outrage face, lips pressed tight, eyes flashing.

Matheus said to his father, "Here he is. I knew he was behind all this." He went to stand behind his father alongside Marcus. Both brothers scowled. "You gave me your word. Some noble you are. Your word is worth nothing. How you managed in Rome is beyond me. We're not happy you are back. Your family is trouble."

Bartholomaeus glanced at Matheus, released Maria's arm, roughly thrusting it away.

Down the passageway to the *peristylum,* Argolicus saw Bishop Braga surrounded by several deacons. He paced in his stiff-gaited way up and down, trailed by his retinue, along the marble pathway next to spring flowers in the garden. The fracas with Maria had interrupted whatever the argument was he'd had with Bartholomaeus.

Before Bartholomaeus could respond, Amalina spoke, her eyes

flashing blue ice but her voice calm. "No, he was against this. It was my idea. My idea to keep a woman from being traumatized, threatened, and hit. You may think of us as barbarians and heretics, but women have an equal place with men." She stood tall, her clear words without rancor.

There was silence. Argolicus marveled at his mother's aplomb, startled and grateful for her intervention. In the far room, he saw Bishop Braga stop his pacing to listen as his deacons stopped speaking, ears turned toward the *atrium*.

Then Bartholomaeus answered. "Whatever you are. Whatever your beliefs. You cannot meddle in our family affairs." He turned to Argolicus. "You go away to Rome and think you can come back and fix everything by trying to control other people's lives. I am *pater familias* here. What I do in my family is my prerogative. I am a true believer, following the traditions of the true church. Women have their place, and men lead. I lead. Maria is marrying into a good family. She is blessed. A spinster like her needs to marry..."

Argolicus had heard enough. He held out his hand. "Mother, come. We can do nothing here."

Amalina crossed to Argolicus and took his hand. He could feel her trembling with anger. He gripped her hand to reassure her and felt the anger throbbing in her palm. But, before he left, he had more to say.

"Maria, I will keep my word." He hoped she understood that he meant to continue looking for Lucas' murderer. She looked at him as she rubbed her arm. He thought he saw a slight nod. He turned to Bartholomaeus. "I will keep my word. I will not meddle in your family affairs."

Bartholomaeus stood as still as a statue. Beyond him in the *peristylum,* Braga and the deacons had stopped any pretense of not listening, their eyes glued on Argolicus.

Holding his mother's hand and followed by Nikolaos, Argolicus strode toward the door.

Outside, they headed back toward the meadow. Amalina trembled in rage.

"What a disgusting man," she said. "He hit Maria. I saw him." She shook her head. "Your father was a Roman. He was nothing like that." She wrapped her *palla* around her shoulders. The blue shawl matched the color of her eyes but not the icy glare.

"I've seen truly evil men in Rome. Yes, Father was exceptional, and we are fortunate. But, Bartholomaeus is full of himself and misguided. Unpleasant but not evil."

"He feels evil to me. What happened to that *civitas* Romans are so proud of? That's an older tradition than the church. It feels like Bartholomaeus picks the traditions that serve his sense of himself. Proud and rigid without courtesy." She was far from calming down. "And what about our own king's *civilitas* where we all are to live in harmony? What about that?"

"Mother, we are far from Ravenna. You see in everyday life here that what the king says has little sway on common occurrences. We were fortunate. I was fortunate to have you and Father. You were fortunate to marry a man who believed in those values. Bartholomaeus isn't like Father. Most men are not like Father was.:

"That man is a brute," Amalina said, rubbing her arm as if to rid herself of the man. Her *palla* slipped, and she pulled it around her again.

"People's beliefs lead them down strange paths of righteousness. Self-righteousness. That's Bartholomaeus. Evil people believe in their twisted thinking that they are doing the right thing. But he isn't evil. He's misguided in his thinking. I've met evil people. They care for no one. Bartholomaeus cares for his family, just in his way. Now,, where is that path to the meadow?"

"Over there," Nikolaos said, pointing to the thick greenery of the woods. He led them into the shadowy woods, where twigs crackled under their feet as they walked.

MEADOW CROSSING

In the darkening woods, Argolicus, Amalina, and Nikolaos trode in defeat toward the meadow and Wiliarit.

"Was it bad judgment?" Amalina asked. "I was trying to protect her. I think all I did was make it worse."

Argolicus sighed. "No, Mother. A caring heart is not bad judgment. But interfering in family matters doesn't work. I supported you, knowing full well that intervention is intrusion. Our families are not destined to be on friendly terms."

"If anything, we've widened the gap," Amalina said. "Harboring Maria was a noble intent but a bad idea."

"We've spent years without contact. Now we can go back to not interacting with the family. I have one last task, and then…"

"What do you mean *one last task*? Didn't you just agree that we'll keep our families separate?"

"I gave my word to Maria. I must find who killed Lucas."

Nikolaos kept silent, leading the way through the thick underbrush. The shadows grew deeper as the afternoon headed toward dusk. They walked on until they could see the sunlight on the flower-filled meadow.

Wiliarit sat cross-legged on the ground, intent on the same star-shaped tiny red flower. Nikolaos cried a greeting. Wiliarit began putting his brushes and paints back in his box.

"I wondered when you'd…" He looked behind Argolicus and Amalina. "Where's Maria?"

"It's a long story. Remember how at the beginning, you warned me not to get involved?" Argolicus said. "You were right. I'll tell you as we walk."

He heard a twig break and turned around. Three hooded ruffians broke out of the woods just as Nikolaos cried, "Hup!"

Argolicus centered his weight on flexed knees as he felt energy surge through his body. It was as if all his senses were on alert. Without thinking, his fingers tingled. He heard each of the hooligans' quiet footsteps. His heart beat in strong, intense rhythm. Wiliarit put down his paint box and reached into his robe. He looked at Argolicus with wide eyes and nodded.

Nikolaos moved first, hurtling through the air toward the first thug. He clung to the huge man. The tutor's feet left the ground as he sent blows up to the thug's face.

Argolicus rushed toward the second hooded figure shaking a club in threatening gestures, his arms up in defense and ready to send out the first punch. Argolicus stopped, stepped forward to put his weight behind his punch to the man's abdomen. The man doubled up with an "oof" of surprise. Jolted by the blow, he dropped the wooden club and leaned in to punch back. His arm didn't reach Argolicus, who danced back, preparing his next strike. The thug moved closer. Argolicus was ready with his defenses. He ducked below the blow, then warded off the next blow with his left arm while landing another punch to the man's jaw with his right fist.

Nikolaos leaped off the big man. Dashed behind and leaped on again, throwing his arm around the big man's neck in a stranglehold. With his other arm, he punched the man repeatedly in the ear and side of his head. The thug leaned over in pain. He tried to shake off the slave. Nikolaos held on and continued his relentless blows to the head.

Wiliarit pulled out a leather-wrapped sap that swung from a leather strap and headed toward the third thug who brandished a club above his head. The thug was unprepared for the reach and swing of the metal-filled leather weapon in the large monk's hand. Wiliarit struck the man's arm held high with the club. A crack resounded through the meadow as the leather sap hit.

Somehow the thug hit Argolicus on his left side. A sear of pain shot through his ribs. He punched back blindly. Unphased, the thug tried a second blow to his side. This time Argolicus had his arm ready to block the blow. And he gained control of his senseless punching to land a blow squarely on the man's jaw. The thug stepped back, shook his head, and fell to the ground.

Amalina was by his side. "Enough of this man. I'll help Wiliarit. You go to Nikolaos." She pulled a long dagger from her belt as she rushed to Wiliarit.

Wiliarit and the thug were grappling in a wrestle on the ground, each man trying to strangle the other.

Argolicus charged toward the large thug with Nikolaos on his back. The thug tried to punch Nikolaos, but the small slave clung behind his head where the man couldn't reach. Argolicus hit him first with his right fist. He followed with a jab from his left to the man's jaw. Stunned, the thug staggered back. Before Argolicus could think, Nikolaos let go. He rushed to the man's front and delivered a blow to the middle of the man's chest. The air rushed out as the man fell to the ground, stunned. He looked up in amazement at the tiny slave in front of him as he gasped for breath.

Amalina tossed the dagger to her left hand. She picked up the leather sap lying beside the two wrestling men. She swung the sap in the air from the leather strap. She stood over the writhing figures and waited for the thug to move within reach. Then she swung the weighted sap on the man's head. He collapsed under Wiliarit.

Amalina ran toward her *palla,* piled in a heap on the meadow grass. She ripped long strips from the shawl. Argolicus realized what she was doing. He took a strip and tied the hands of the thug who had fought Wiliarit. When he was finished, he bound the big thug who had not been able shake off Nikolaos. Amalina ripped more strips. Finally, Argolicus bound the hands of the thug who had passed out from the blow to the jaw.

"Now," said Argolicus, standing over the three men. "Who sent you?"

The two who were conscious spoke together.

"It was a man…"

"He didn't give us his name…"

"One at a time," Argolicus said.

Wiliarit was up from the ground. Amalina handed him the sap. "Useful tool, brother." Wiliarit smiled.

Argolicus waited. None of the three men spoke. Argolicus pointed at the largest thug. "Tell me."

"He was… he didn't say his name. He… he had money."

"He gave you money to find us?"

"Yes, he said you would come toward the meadow."

The third thug woke up, sat up, shook his head, and stared at his bound hands.

"And, what did he want you to do?"

"You. He described you. Noble with a monk and a woman from The People."

"And?"

"You. He told us to get rid of you. He promised more money when we returned."

Wiliarit put his arm around Amalina. She leaned onto his shoulder.

"Describe this man," Argolicus continued.

"He was a slave, like that little devil there." He pointed to Nikolaos. "Well dressed. A clean tunic. Medium tall. Brown hair. Ordinary house slave."

"Who sent him?"

"He… he didn't say."

"And, where were you? How did he know how to find you?

"We're always outside the bishop's palace. You know how it is. No steady work. But sometimes we get jobs."

"Like this one?"

"Well, not exactly like this one. Usually, it's, you know, someone who owes the bishop. We go to collect." He nodded toward the other two thugs.

"Have you ever done something like this before?"

The thug looked down, then glanced at the other two.

"Well... not all three of us."

"What do you mean not all three? Just you?"

"I'm the biggest. I..."

"I see." Argolicus felt he was close to a revelation. "Recently? Recently anything like this?"

The thug looked out at the forest trees, over at Wiliarit's paint box, down at his feet. He mumbled, "Just one."

"Here, in this meadow?"

"How did you...? You couldn't..."

"Here. In this meadow?"

"Y,.. Y,.. Yes. Just one man. A poor one. I did what I was asked."

"Which was?"

"Bring back his bag. Hurt him." The big thug shifted on the ground.

"And you did? You hurt him and took back the bag."

The thug shifted his eyes and said, "Yes. Hurt him. Then grabbed the bag and ran."

"You did more than hurt him."

The thug nodded his head and looked away at the trees again. "I heard. I didn't mean... It just happened."

"I want to understand," Argolicus said. "You were not told to kill him?"

"He didn't use the word. No. But, he..." The thug searched for a word.

"He implied. He meant that hurting could be killing."

"Yes, yes. You understand. I mean, I hardly ever get instructions to kill. But people, some people, know I can rough people up. And, what was that word?"

"Imply."

"Yes, sometimes the instructions imply."

A breeze rustled in the trees. The grass and flowers nodded in the meadow. Everyone was silent, waiting for Argolicus to decide. Argolicus felt like hitting the man. But he checked himself because the man was just a thug, and not a smart one. He needed to know who had hired the thug.

"This man, the man who gave you the instructions. Tell me more about him. Anything you remember. Anything at all."

The man shook his head. "He was just a slave. I told you."

"He had good shoes," the thug in front of Amalina said, eyeing her dagger.

"Good shoes? What do you mean?" Argolicus asked, turning toward the man. He didn't know what this meant, but maybe it was something.

"They weren't fancy, no embroidery, but they were good shoes. New leather. Supple. No blisters for that man." The thug looked at his feet out in front of him. "See these? Stiff. Even though they're worn, they are stiff. But that slave is taken care of. I can tell you that. I used to work leather before these hard times. Those shoes were good shoes."

"Anything else?"

The three men looked at each other.

The big thug shrugged his shoulders. "He was from here. I guess that just adds to his being ordinary. You know how slaves come from all over the world? Well, this one had no accent. He looked like us... well, except for being better dressed. I mean, he was just an ordinary man but from Bruttium. He was easy to understand."

Argolicus was getting bits and pieces but nothing that distinguished the man who had paid the thugs. "Alright, let's get you to the pro-magistrate. Nikolaos, lead the way."

Amalina loosened the ties around the thugs' feet to hobble them. Wiliarit got the men to stand up one by one. Argolicus gathered the thugs' clubs and wrapped them in what was left of Amalina's shawl, so it served as a large bag. Then they all headed through the woods toward home. The sun was getting low in the sky. The trees cast dark shadows, and Argolicus was glad Nikolaos knew the way.

At the villa, they gathered the men in the courtyard until the pro-magistrate arrived. A kitchen slave came out with soup for everyone. Another slave set up torch lights around the courtyard against the gathering evening. They waited in silence.

As the shock of the attack wore off, and they were all safe at home with the thugs apprehended, Argolicus felt the pains of the attack and muscle soreness from fighting. The knuckles on both hands ached. A dull pain burned his left shoulder, and his ribs ached. But, what bothered him was his frustration at finding the person who had instigated the attack and, now that he knew, Lucas' murder. They had apprehended the thugs, but he didn't know the person with the intent. The men in front of him were merely living instruments, like the clubs they had wielded.

He glanced at Wiliarit, who had a red welt on his cheek. Amalina's pale cheeks seemed to highlight the lines around her mouth and eyes. Nikolaos, standing by the practice swords they'd used this morning, was rubbing his arm. The practice swords. Without that constant practice, Argolicus would have been unprepared for the attack. The king's law forbade Romans from carrying arms. Only The People could carry arms. He'd been fortunate to have his mother and Wiliarit with him... and prepared. More than fortunate that Nikolaos made him practice. Suddenly, he had a sense of how they could have ended up left in the meadow like Lucas.

He heard horses approaching and men's voices. The pro-magistrate and his deputies appeared in the courtyard. They rounded up the three thugs. As they led them away, the big thug turned around. "He had a missing tooth... on the bottom."

PAINTING A NEW PICTURE

The figures on the frescos seemed to move in the flickering lamplight in the *triclinium*. Reclining on the dining bench relaxed Argolicus' sore muscles, and the food on the table smelled delicious.

"I was ravenous," Wiliarit said, dipping a spoon into the herbed lentil soup. They spoke in Their Language since it was only the three of them. "It's been a long time since I've been in a fight." He rubbed at a cut over his eye.

Argolicus laughed. "I haven't had a real fight since boyhood. This was different. They planned to harm us. I don't think killing was out of the question. As the man said, it was implied." His raw knuckles stretched in pain as he lifted his spoon.

"But why?" Amalina asked, signaling for the next dish. "Was helping Maria worth killing? That family. Bartholomaeus is not a nice man. Killing us wouldn't accomplish anything. He has his daughter back." Argolicus looked at the rough patch on her cheek that would soon be a large scab. The wrinkles that radiated from the corners of her eyes, always associated with smiles, indicated that age was not a barrier to courage.

"I don't know," Argolicus said. "I've sent a message to him that Lucas' killer is apprehended and with the promagistrate in town. He will have to resolve it in his own way. But for us, it doesn't solve the problem. If someone wants us out of the way, they can hire different thugs. We haven't found the real murderer. The one who had Lucas killed. The one who sent thugs after us." He tried shifting away from the aches again without success.

"Ah, tuna," Wiliarit said, as the fish in lovage and mint sauce arrived on the table. He put down his spoon and waited as the kitchen slave put a steaming piece of fish on a plate. "Do you think it's personal, against us, or some provincial rebellion against The People?" He tucked into the tuna with vigorous bites.

"In some ways it doesn't matter," Argolicus said. "A threat is a threat. And Mother is right. Why? I suspect it has something to do with Lucas. But what? What we do know is that Lucas is dead, the icon is missing, and we were attacked." He shifted on the couch trying to get comfortable, but the aches just shifted with his movement.

"That poor girl," Amalina said, taking a larger than usual portion of fish. "When is her wedding? She can't get away from all that fast enough."

"You were the one that talked to her. I thought you knew. Isn't it in a few weeks?" Argolicus felt his obligation pressing in. He might never keep his promise to Maria.

Amalina nodded her head. "It can't be soon enough."

"We will stay away from that family," Argolicus said. "I'll keep looking for who wanted Lucas dead because they threatened us, too. But, unless we determine that a family member hired those thugs, we stay away." A bitterness rose in his throat. How old allegiances had come back to strike him and his family.

Amalina and Wiliarit nodded.

"Where is Nikolaos?"

"Now that dinner has been prepared, he's busy in the kitchen, cooking up remedies for us," Amalina replied, her cheek stretching with the stiff red patch.

"Ugh," Wiliarit said. "I hope we don't have to drink some vile concoction from his herb garden."

"Those vile concoctions work," Argolicus said in defense of his tutor. "He knows plants. Isn't that why you are here?"

"Yes, yes." Wiliarit conceded. "But still..."

"Do you want to wait to have the fruit?" Amalina asked with complete deadpan, summoning years of sibling communication.

"No, no. Fruit next," Wiliarit said. "We can drink honeyed wine after any of Nikolaos' potions."

After dinner, Nikolaos gathered them all on the benches in

the *peristylum*. The night was warm for late March. Slaves lit up the area with torches.

Nikolaos had prepared poultices for wounds and, yes, a tangy, but not bitter, herbal tisane for them all. In the quiet moments, while his patients were under his care, he pulled out a book and began reading. "*Nature is pliable, obedient. And the logos that governs it has no reason to do evil. It knows no evil, does none, and causes harm to nothing. It dictates all beginnings and all endings.*" He paused, glanced at all the visible wounds, and continued. "*Just that you do the right thing. The rest doesn't matter.*"

"I could do the right thing now, rest," Wiliarit said, interrupting the reading and speaking in Latin for the benefit of Nikolaos. "But what burns my mind is who hired those thugs." He touched the poultice over his wound. "They did this, but their intent was worse."

Argolicus nodded raising his soaking knuckles with the cup to sip the tisane. Not as vile as expected.

"Think of them all," Argolicus said. "Bartholomaeus, Braga, Mattheus, Marcus, why would they really care about the icon? What upset them all was his new belief. The way he countered the traditions and hierarchies of the Church by supporting a belief system that had to do with personal decisions. Lucas was a defiant departure from tradition." Somehow, sitting on the bench made his aches feel better. The dining couch. He wondered about sleep in bed. Would it be as uncomfortable as reclining to eat?

"I agree," Amalina said, taking a sip of tisane and making a face. "Nikolaos, what is this?"

"Surely, it's time for some honeyed wine," Wiliarit said, taking a gulp of tisane to make it disappear.

"Have you finished your drink?" Nikolaos asked, looking up from the book. His instruction from Marcus Aurelius was not keeping anyone's attention. He closed the book.

Everyone nodded yes.

Wiliarit tipped up his cup for one last sip. Then he set the cup down. "It wasn't as awful as I'd expected."

Nikolaos ignored him and continued, "Each of them has enough money to hire a thug, even a band of thugs, to do their dirty work. Since we know the same thugs were used against Lucas and against us, we only need to find the one person behind them."

"Well, that goes without saying," Argolicus replied, feeling irritable with his aching body and scored knuckles. "But, I will not give up."

Wiliarit said, "I think I know. Well, I have a strong suspicion."

They all looked at him expectantly. A servant brought out a tray with cups and a pitcher of honeyed wine.

"Ah, inspiration," Wiliarit said, reaching for a cup.

"Don't make us wait, Uncle. Tell us your idea."

"It's like the sketches I've been doing. You have a subject, in this case, all the people who might have wished Lucas harm, but when you start the next sketch, you see a detail that had escaped your notice before..."

"Stop," Amalina said in her older sister voice. "Skip the theoretical analogy and get to your idea."

"Let me put it less artistically," Wiliarit continued without missing a beat. "Solving a puzzle, like who killed Lucas, isn't so much about finding tidbits of clues that can point in any direction. It's about knowing what to look for. And, you may scoff," he looked at Amalina, "but it's like painting a new picture of the same subject."

Argolicus, determined to quell a decades-old sibling squabble, said, "Paint the picture."

"We've been focused on Church traditions and how Lucas antagonized everyone with his newfound faith. But we've overlooked something equally strong, the hierarchy inside the Church. Instead of looking at which Church or Church leader holds the correct belief, we can look at the structure inside the Church. I work with this structure when I make books for prelates."

"I don't understand," Nikolaos said as he peeked under Amalina's poultice to check her wound.

"We've been basing our thoughts on the outside traditions, but we need to look at the inside traditions. You can't imagine how complicated it is in Constantinople. Rome is nothing. And, here, for Squillace, the structure is the same."

Argolicus could see his mother was about to reprimand Wiliarit again. He spoke before she could. "Explain. I'm not sure I understand either."

"Unlike a priest, loyal to the Church, the deacon's obligation is to the bishop. If the bishop orders something, the deacon performs. Braga could express a wish or even mumble a discontent, and a zealous deacon eager for advancement who heard him could carry out an act unknown to the bishop. Braga need not be involved personally. The deacon might mention later an act he had done in order to curry favor and gain personal prestige with the bishop. This is the picture. While priests are bound to the Church, deacons are bound by oath to serve the bishop. Theoretically, they carry out the benevolence of the bishop through daily actions. They perform administrative duties, like a merchant's clerks. And if the bishop expresses a desire, they make it happen in the everyday world."

"So, the man with the missing tooth came from a deacon, not the bishop?" Amalina asked, sipping at her cup of wine.

"The bishop, but through a deacon. The man with the missing tooth never spoke to the bishop. He received an order and carried it out. All this could happen without the bishop's knowledge. Of course, this is a speculative thought."

Nikolaos approached Wiliarit to check his wound, but the monk waved him away. The monk took a long sip of wine.

"That's an interesting theory, but why couldn't he come from someone in Bartholomaeus' family? I don't see how we've narrowed it down to the bishop or a deacon," Amalina said, determine to poke a hole in her brother's elaborate analogy.

Nikolaos fussed with Argolicus knuckles, patting the poultice around the edges. Argolicus winced. They still went in circles around Lucas' murder.

"So, let's start with the Bishop. We can't go to Bartholomaeus' house. Truthfully, I don't want to see him again. Uncle, can you make one last visit before you leave for Constantinople?"

Wiliarit nodded, then took a gulp of honeyed wine.

Wiliarit took time out from sketching plants to paint a representation of Ignatius of Antioch sailing on a boat to Rome writing letters to his flock.

"Usually, he's represented with the lions grinding his bones, but Braga doesn't seem like a man who wants to think about martyrdom."

"It's ready?" Argolicus asked. "And you have an appointment?"

"Yes, this afternoon."

"Thank you for doing this, Uncle. We have no idea if this will reveal anything at all."

"You gave your word to Maria. Plus, I know you. You don't give up." He put his large arm around Argolicus' shoulder.

* * *

This time there was no visit to the treasures. Braga met them in the sparse *salutorium*. Seated on his bishop's chair, he listened to Wiliarit as he displayed his painting of Ignatius. Wiliarit handed the vellum sheet with the image to the bishop.

"So, the book would have the letters of Ignatius written in a fine script with illustrations, much like this one. You can control the price in accordance with how many illustrations you want added to the letters."

Braga squinted at the sheet, his stubby ringed fingers handling the sheet with care. With his other hand, he motioned to several deacons standing at the side of the big empty room. "You have read this Ignatius?"

The answers came back in mumbles. "No." "I don't read, Father." "No, but it would be a worthy addition."

A young deacon came into the room, brown robes hanging over a thin frame. "Your visitor." He announced.

Braga frowned, his snub nose wrinkling. "He is early. But bring him in."

The deacon returned, followed by Bartholomaeus. He swept in with his silks flowing. Frowned at Argolicus and Wiliarit, went to the bishop, fell on his knee, and kissed the bishop's ring snuggled among the jeweled fingers.

The bishop said, "Let me finish here. I'm considering adding a book to the collection." He held out the vellum sheet to Bartholomaeus.

"For your library?" Bartholomaeus asked. "What will it be? Who is this?" He pointed to the figure on the boat.

While the bishop told Bartholomaeus about the early Church fathers and Ignatius in particular, Argolicus looked at the deacons arranged around the room. Was Wiliarit right? Could the murderous plotter be one of them? They all looked just as committed as Wiliarit did in his monk's robes. If it was one of the deacons, how would he discover which one? Had he set himself up for a fool's errand? And, now, Bartholomaeus was here. There was bound to be trouble.

The entry door opened again. This time a servant entered, not a deacon. With soft steps not to disturb the bishop, he sidled around the edges of the room until he stood by a deacon. Argolicus recognized the deacon as the one who had taken them on the tour of the treasures. What was his name? Mico. Yes. And now he was in a whispered conversation with a servant, a servant with very nice shoes, Argolicus noticed. The whispered conversation continued. Braga looked at them briefly, scowled, and then continued with his explanation. The servant smiled, exposing his teeth, and turned to leave.

"Your Grace," Argolicus interrupted. "With your permission, could I have a word?"

Braga stopped. Argolicus saw his face pass from annoyance to curiosity back to annoyance. A strand of his oiled hair had escaped over his forehead as he bent over the sketch. He pushed it back.

"Yes," Braga said. "Is it about the book? I think I have made my decision."

"No," Argolicus answered as he walked toward the deacon Mico. "I have a question for your deacon."

Mico squirmed in his plain robe, glanced at the servant, and left his spot by the wall. "Yes?"

But Braga cut them short. "What is it? I was just getting ready to give the talented monk his answer."

Argolicus, with no explanation, turned to the deacon. "This is your servant?"

The servant tried to keep his composure but sent a worried glance at Mico, who answered, "He belongs to the palace... all of us."

Argolicus turned to the servant. "This man," he pointed to the deacon, "gave you money to hire men outside the palace?"

The servant glanced down, up at the deacon Mico, and down again. "Many times."

"And the last two times?"

Bartholomaeus spoke up. "What's this about? You seem to meddle wherever you go."

Argolicus pointed to the servant, who seemed to want to disappear. "This, as you say, *this* man and this deacon," he turned to Mico, "are about the death of your son."

Braga dropped the sketch. "What is he saying, Mico?"

"Is this true? How?" Bartholomaeus asked.

"Your Grace," Mico said, casting his eyes down. "I heard you. I heard you say what a pestilence that man was, how you wanted him to disappear."

"What are you saying?" Braga stood, his face flushed red. "You hired men in my name to kill that young man?"

"Not in your name," Mico answered, his voice rising. "I hoped to make your desire a fact. I wanted to please you. I thought you would..."

Bartholomaeus strode across the empty *salutorium*. He hit the deacon and then the servant. Then he pummeled the deacon. "You! My son! My boy. You. You. You." With each word, he struck Mico, who fell to the floor. Bartholomaeus lifted his leg to kick.

"Enough," Braga said, his voice filling the big room. Bartholomaeus stood back, his face filled with fury. "Mico, you have dishonored your calling, my name, and the Church. You are no longer bound to the duties and obligations you incurred upon ordination. Go, take off your robes and wait in the entry room for the pro-magistrate. And, you," he turned to the servant whose mouth, open in stunned surprise, showed his missing tooth, "you will go with this man and wait with him for the pro-magistrate."

The two men slunk from the room. The bishop returned to his ornate chair. The other deacons stood silently, their faces filled with mixtures of surprise, condemnation, and shame. Bartholomaeus stood with a similar combination of surprise and shame.

"Your Grace, I must put off our business for today."

Braga nodded. "There is no rush. We have time and faith to begin our project. May your soul be at peace with this new knowledge."

Wiliarit stooped to pick up the vellum sheet. He handed it back to the bishop.

Bartholomaeus turned to Argolicus. "You accomplished something I prayed for every day, the discovery of who killed Lucas. Our faiths will always separate us, but I will always be in your debt."

"Tell Maria I kept my word."

***

Days later, the carter loaded boxes onto a cart as Amalina and Wiliarit hugged their goodbyes. Wiliarit let go of his sister.

"Nikolaos, forays with you helped me complete all my sketches. Your knowledge," he shook his head. "I would have been lost without it. And, you," he said, turning to Argolicus. "Our peaceful discussions turned into something quite lively. City life will seem calm after this." He held his arms wide open and then embraced Argolicus. He pushed back and said to the carter, "Ready."

As he settled into the seat beside the carter, he said to Argolicus, "I left something for you on your desk" The carter called to the horses, and they were off down the hill.

In his study, Argolicus found a sheet of vellum with an inscription surrounded by small, red, yellow, and blue meadow flowers. *Do the right thing. The rest does not matter.*

"Mother," he called. "Your brother is astounding."

Amalina appeared at the door. "He is. But now it's time to talk about what you will do with the rest of your life."

Argolicus sighed.

Wiliarit's book, The Dioscorides was translated into Latin with the title De Materia Medica. The book in the story is the oldest extant copy and was presented the Emperor Anicius Olybrius' daughter, Juliana Anica, around 512 C.E. The book is currently housed in the Austrian National Library in Vienna. The book includes hundreds of illustrations some of which occupy Wiliarit in the story.

Although Wiliarit is credited with the creation of The Gothic Bible (Codex Argenteus at Uppsala University) and other books of the time, he is not directly connected with the Dioscorides. I imagined him creating the book and needing Nikolaos' help.

According to Patrick Amory's *People and identity in Ostrogothic Italy 480-554*, Wiliarit was probably a monk as well as a book maker. I reduced the probability to a certainty and created his familial relationship with Argolicus.

At the time of the story, monks, both Arian and Trini- tarian, either lived alone or in loose communities based on the tradition of the Desert Fathers like Anthony. At this time, Benedict lived alone in a cave following that tradition. He had yet to form his monastery or create his Rules. His connection with Lucas comes from my imagination.

Modern readers should understand that religion and poli- tics were intertwined. Feelings ran strong about the nature of Christ and colored daily activities and interactions in a way it's difficult to comprehend today.

The Henotikon was a document issued by the Emperor Zeno in 491 C.E. in an attempt to unify the various sects (heresies) of the Christian Church. It caused a schism between East and West and was not settled until 519 C.E. seven years after the time of this story. Bartholomaeus may seem extreme, but he was current. His iron fist over his family was within his rights as paterfamilias.

Amalina's feelings about women come from her Ostrogoth heritage where women had equal rights with men, within tribal law.

According to James J. O'Donnell in, The Ruin of the Roman Empire, the most upwardly mobile sector at this time were members of the Church. Braga is a man of his times.

I am grateful to James J. O'Donnell for his personal encouragement when I first began my journey with Argolicus and the reign of Theoderic.

Historical fiction is built on a combination of history and the author's imagination. All historical errors are mine and mine alone.

Zara Altair

THE PEACH WIDOW

A MOTHER'S WISH

Argolicus left his cool studio to walk into the garden, where the air instantly warmed his cheeks. A clatter came from the kitchen. A kitchen worker of about 14, bore a tray of fruit and a pitcher of milk and honey toward a table set out by the fountain. Argolicus' mother sat at the table in front of hot, thin bread rounds and a glass pot of honey with a silver dipper. She was a tall, striking woman in her early fifties and bore her Ostrogoth heritage with the straight shoulders and uplifted chin of a Roman matron. Braids of golden hair, here and there streaked with gray, wound around her head like a crown. Dressed for a day of work managing the estate, she wore a long light tunic of woven flax.

"Good morning," she smiled and looked up from her notes.

"'Morning," Argolicus waited, standing as a young girl brought out a chair for him to sit. He reached for a peach from the fruit tray.

"Ah, ripe peaches at last."

"Argolicus, the widow Valerius…"

"Mother, please. Wait until I've eaten."

She drew out a parchment scrap and began scratching away

making notes to herself about the busy summer day ahead running the estate.

The fountain burbled happily in the morning sunlight as Argolicus silently used a knife to section the peach and withdraw the pit. Juice ran over his fingers onto the plate. He dipped his fingers in a bowl of orange water, shook his hands over the ground, and then poured a cup of milk and honey. As he sipped, he mentally planned his work for the day in the cool study hidden away from the hot July sun.

The peach was so delicious, he started sectioning another.

"Yes, the widow Valerius?"

"Her stepsons." His mother looked up from her tablet. "I didn't quite understand it all. You are so much better at legalities; I thought maybe you could help."

"Help what?"

"Settle the dispute. Isn't that what you did in Rome?"

"Mother, I'm retired. Why doesn't she seek the regular channels? We have a governor."

"Venantius? You should know. Remember how he treated Adeodatus? Imagine being a widow of not much means. She has land but not much money. How would she ingratiate herself? You know he wants monetary favors. If you want to settle in here, you can help our neighbors."

"Yes, Venantius is not impartial. Money or land, given freely, help him make decisions."

Argolicus sighed. Even the country was tainted by politics. "Dispute? What dispute?"

"Her stepsons want her to leave. She would be penniless. I'm remembering how I felt when your father died. I had this place and you and still felt completely alone. I can't imagine what it would be like to be thrust out into the world as a woman with no family."

Argolicus reached out and touched her shoulder. "Mother, I like you close. I will go see your widow."

He found himself, on an even hotter day, up before sunrise. Accompanied by Nikolaos, his Greek tutor, secretary, and companion, he quietly rode the five miles to the villa Valerius. As they reached the top of a grade and began their descent into the valley, port and ocean disappeared from view, the bustle and commerce of the city abandoned for the quiet isolation of rural life.

The estate spread across a small valley surrounded by hills. A stream, bordered by green willows and rose-laurel, ran down from the hills, cutting a seam through the fields of grass turning gold in the sun. The pink flowers of the bushes were alive with color in the otherwise dry golds and grays of the hot summer day. Beyond the farm's complex of buildings, fruit trees grew in rows that stretched to the foothills, orange peaches poking out beneath the green leaves. Their horses slogged along as if they had traveled a long distance without rest. Nikolaos seemed unfazed by the heat, but Argolicus could see his tunic was already sticking to his back. Even though the day had just begun, the sun was already merciless heat.

Once they passed the thick walls of the villa and entered the vestibule, the air was cool. A young man in his mid-twenties waited for them in the atrium. He struck Argolicus as middling throughout. His height was moderate, his face plain but not ugly, his hair a nondescript brown. His heavy linen tunic was plain with no embroidery.

"Welcome, Your Illustrious Sublimity. Secundus Valerius. My mother will join us shortly. I'm so glad you are here." His voice was moderate, but in no way obsequious. Argolicus decided he was a plain-spoken farmer who seemed to know basic protocol.

A slave hurried across the atrium from the back of the villa and whispered, just loud enough for Argolicus to hear, "Your mother waits in the atrium."

Secundus waved his arm to a passageway, inviting Argolicus to follow. "This way. She waits in the garden."

Nikolaos trailed behind as they made their way into the garden. And, amazingly the garden was cool. An old plane tree, filled with the broad leaves for which it was named, created a leafy covering which cooled the garden. A fountain splashed quietly, surrounded by sweet, scented herbs. Several chairs were grouped by the tree's vast trunk near a small table. The widow sat in one of the chairs gazing at the fountain.

"Mother," Secundus said. "Your guest is here."

She turned and smiled. It was a smile from long ago, a bit of a flirt, her chest out, her eyes widened, her teeth white and even. The smile of a coquette on a body much older.

"Livilla Valerius, Your Sublimity," she said, not dropping the smile. Her hair was dark with slight touches of gray at the temples, combed up and pinned in a fashion current in Rome when he left. She stretched out a plump arm and gestured to a chair. "I took my husband's name when we married. Thank you for coming. I admire your mother greatly. She is wise."

"She is," Argolicus replied, taking her warm hand and then dropping it. "She tells me..."

"Yes, I talked to her. Secundus," she said, turning to the son, "find Tatius. We will eat together in a while with our guest."

Nikolaos leaned against the trunk of the plane tree, his eyes focused on a middle distance, his tablet and stylus ready for notes. The widow Livilla did not look at him.

Secundus left, and a young woman, with astounding brown eyes and, as animal breeders say, perfect conformation, brought a bowl of fruit and some light wine.

Livilla turned to Argolicus, posing with her head tilted above a shoulder, turned in his direction. "Amalina, your mother, she said you could help. I am grateful."

"My mother gives me more credit than is due. I can't promise I can help. As you know, I have no official capacity. I can use my experience to make suggestions. Your husband, what happened?"

"He was a good man. And so strong and vigorous. I just...the way he died. Like an old man. We were out here in the garden after dinner."

"What do you mean 'like an old man'?"

"We were sitting. Well, we weren't exactly sitting." She gave another coquettish smile. "All of a sudden, his heart. He felt sick. Then he clutched his chest. He kept saying, 'I can't stop it.' He gasped for air. He doubled over." She choked and gasped. She wrung her hands emphasizing her distress. "Then he fell on the ground. I called for Tatius and Secundus, but he was already gone. I miss him every day. But that's not the problem," Livilla shook her head. "Now Tatius wants everything. He controls the activities here. He wants me gone." Her voice cracked. A tear glistened at the corner of her left eye. "I don't understand. He was always a headstrong boy, but now..."

Argolicus was losing patience with her ramblings. No wonder his mother had such a difficult time explaining. "Livilla Valerius, help me understand the situation. You have your dowry and your marriage deposit, yes?"

"Yes, yes. That's not it. And I want to stay here. Secundus says..."

"And neither of the sons are yours? They were born to your husband's first wife?"

"Yes, that's true. But Secundus is like my own. He was only a small child, not even two years old, when I married. He thinks of me as his mother."

"What about Tatius?"

"Tatius has changed." She gave him another smile, but it was only half as flirtatious as the first. He saw how once she had been beautiful, as his own Julia had been beautiful, petite with clear skin and flowing dark hair. But now, even though her tunica was fine linen and richly embroidered, the ties around her bodice and waist only accentuated how she had filled out to roundness. She breathed in, blew out the air in a puff, and continued.

"He is mean. Sometimes he says he wants Secundus to leave, too." She leaned forward to find a plum in the bowl. Argolicus watched her breasts sway underneath the soft fabric, and immediately eluded the inviting glance she gave him. "Would you care for a plum? Or a peach?" Livilla asked in a welcoming hostess voice.

"No, thank you. Tatius?" He was finding the widow Valerius, and particularly her coquettish ways that belie her plump, middle-aged body, tiresome. He made an effort to push back his personal reaction. He was irritated that he had no clear picture of her situation, which was the reason he was here. He heard Nikolaos scratching on his tablet.

"You will meet him soon. He pokes and emphasizes that he wants me to leave." She paused, took a breath, continued, "I've been here so long...25 years. I don't know another life. He keeps telling me he is not legally bound to take care of me. Is that right?"

"Right or wrong, it is the law. He is correct that he has no legal obligation to you." Argolicus was clear on the law. Inwardly, he felt relieved. "You are not his mother."

"Family," she sighed, as the girlishness was disappeared before his eyes as her shoulders sagged. She looked now like a defeated matron. She started to cry. Nikolaos was scratching away, peering at his tablet, then looking at the garden, then scratching again.

"Livilla Valerius, it is the law, but a very heartless way for a stepson to act. I am sorry."

She looked up. "There is no law to protect me? My dowry was not especially large."

"Only that which returns your dowry and your marriage pledge goods and money. He can't keep that. He must return it..."

"I didn't think it would be like this..."

"Mother," a rough voice called from the portico arch. "Are you whining again? And to a stranger?"

Livilla wiped her eyes as Argolicus stood up. "Gaius Vitellius Argolicus," he said.

"Valerius Tatius." He nodded in greeting. "What is your business?"

Tatius wore a tunic of unbleached linen covered with fruit stains with a large green leaf-stained smudge on the side. He was short and dark, like his mother, with the same blocky body. By his side stood a large dog, broad across the chest, with powerful legs and jaws which looked as though they could crush iron. The dog was entirely white except for a black nose and deep brown eyes focused on Argolicus.

A warm breeze rustled the plane tree leaves. Nikolaos stopped scratching on the tablet. Livilla cringed.

"Pup, down," Tatius said in a quiet voice. The dog dropped to the ground, looking up at Tatius with adoration.

"Tatius," Livilla stood breaking out from her embarrassment. "We are discussing the farm. Tell Argolicus how we do our trade."

Tatius glanced at Livilla, then looked Argolicus in the eye. "The farm is what you see—the orchards, a few livestock, olives. My father loved farming and so do I. But, Livilla, you don't pay much attention to the farm. Why were you talking about the farm?"

"I was telling him how much I like it here," she answered, covering her inheritance concerns.

"Ha!," Tatius grunted. Pup looked up. "You say that, Livilla. Your Sublimity, perhaps we can talk after the meal."

"Yes," Argolicus replied, thinking that it had been Livilla who had requested his counsel. His experience in Rome had brought him face-to-face with aggressive posturing. People were people, so he was not surprised, knowing the best way to deal with this posturing was to ignore it unless it became physical. In reality, he had answered the widow's question. Now, all that was left was to exhibit courtesy and join the family for the meal.

❧   2   ❧

BARGAINS AND PEACHES

Secundus led Argolicus on a tour of the farm while servants prepared the meal. Nikolaos followed behind silently. Outside without the shade of the plane tree, the sun beat mercilessly on their heads. Secundus headed for the barn.

"I find our buyers and make all the arrangements. I go into town to the market and talk to people."

They walked through a gate to the barn's enclosure. Cattle and a couple of horses stomped and swished at flies in their stalls. In the center stood empty sheep corrals and several pens with reclining pigs. The yard and the barn were exceptionally clean, but the heat was ripe with the scent of livestock.

"That is how we established our regular trade with Rome. Tatius likes working the farm. He's good with the animals. They like him." Secundus waved toward the animals in the barn.

"Like Pup?" Argolicus asked.

"Yes, Pup, the horses, even the oxen," Secundus smiled. "It's a gift. For business, we have a good arrangement. Look, here is our barn." He opened the broad doorway to the enclosure. "We have two cows and sell milk to neighbors. And two oxen for pulling carts and heavy work like uprooting tree stumps. Each of us has a horse. I'm looking to breed my mare. I hear you have a beautiful red stallion."

Secundus carefully closed the gate, led the way to the barn, marching across the animal enclosure toward a door in the barn. He opened the door and beckoned Argolicus into the shade of a storeroom. Secundus reached up and grabbed three wide-brimmed straw hats. He handed one to Argolicus and one to Nikolaos as he pointed his chin upward toward the sun.

"Thank you," Argolicus said, placing the hat on his head, thinking how generous Secundus was to give a hat to Nikolaos as well. "Ah, Mercury's Flame. He's quite a handful, but beautiful conformation." Argolicus understood how Secundus made his connections. He was a gifted man of business with his easy manner and ability to get straight to the point, which put his interlocutor at ease. "Get in touch with the overseer Lucius. He'll take care of her while she's in heat."

"Mother had a mare, but she died last spring. I thought the best way would be for us to breed a new horse. We don't have a lot of money..." His voice trailed off. He glanced up at the hills, then turned to Argolicus. "Would you like to see the orchards? We've mostly peaches and some apples that we use here in the fall." He turned around and led them out of the barn's enclosure. Once outside, they started around the barn to the orchards beyond.

"He wasn't a good man," Secundus said, his eyes on the orchard ahead.

Argolicus was baffled for a second.

"He was cruel. He kept treating Mother as though she were a second-class citizen, even though she is a true Roman. You met her. You saw how hard she tries to please...anyone. Anyone and everyone."

They reached the edge of the orchard. Peach trees stretched in long rows ahead of them. Slaves climbed on ladders. They gently picked the fruit and filled cloth slings hanging from their shoulders. When the shoulder sling was full, the workers climbed down the ladder to fill large baskets placed around the orchard.

Argolicus felt a twinge of guilt for his irritation at her behavior. He adjusted the hat, so the brim shaded more of his face. "She does try to please, but..."

"Oh, I know," Secundus said. "She was young when she married our brute of a father and only knows what worked when she was a girl. She may not be great with people, but she is a good mother. She's who I know as Mother."

A group of slaves started singing as they worked the far end of the orchard.

"Your workers seem content," Argolicus commented.

"They work harder now that Father is gone. Tatius works his magic on them. It's the same as it is with the dog; he is kind but strict," Secundus answered. "You know, our father was a real bastard, he used to make us work with the slaves as punishment, but without their food breaks. In harvest season, or when the ewes were lambing, sometimes we worked 14 or 16 hours a day. I don't miss him. I don't miss him at all. But Tatius is a different story."

"Tell me," Argolicus suggested, hoping he would get a full explanation, something to take back to his mother. The singing slaves chanted with full gusto as they worked in the trees.

"Our father was not without skills, his farming knowledge—trees especially—was detailed. As Tatius followed him around, he picked up one tip after another. With Tatius' skill, we're starting to make more money with what we have. Oh, and he has an experiment going on with the peaches. He *borrowed* a cutting from someone in town with a delicious white peach with an astounding flavor. It's like..." he paused trying to think of the right words. "It's like essence of peach concentrated in each bite."

Argolicus nodded recognizing the procedure. Nikolaos took a note.

Secundus continued, "He used an already existing tree, made a cut, and inserted the sprig from the other tree into the cut. Then he wrapped up the tree wound in cloth soaked in oil and herbs and, miraculously, the branch grew and produced those white peaches."

Argolicus interrupted, "Livilla told me that you and Tatius want her to leave. Without getting too personal, why? Why would Tatius throw out his stepmother? And you? You seem to have affection for her. It doesn't make sense to me. I saw inheritance grabs in Rome, but here in the country, I don't understand. She can't be that much of a burden."

Two things happened at the same moment. Pup bounded into the orchard, and the singing abruptly changed to cries of alarm. Tatius followed Pup into the orchard and then ran to the far end where the noise was loudest. Someone was screaming. Secundus, Argolicus, and Nikolaos all ran.

A worker had fallen from a ladder. One of the rungs had broken and pierced his leg just above the ankle.

Nikolaos took one look and said, "I'm going to the herb garden. They have what he needs." He took off at a run toward the villa.

Tatius organized other slaves to intertwine several cloth slings to carry the worker. Then he appointed four slaves to carry the wounded man. He ordered everyone else back to work. The group headed to the barn where they laid the wounded man on clean straw. His cries subsided. Pup thought it was all a game and bounded and cavorted around them until Tatius gave him the same "down" command and down he went on the spot. The young man moaned and then subsided into silence, grimacing in pain.

Nikolaos and Livilla arrived with a steaming pot, strips of cloth, some long fuzzy leaves, and orange flowers. Nikolaos produced a stick from the folds of his clothing and stripped off pieces of bark. "Chew this," he said in vernacular Latin to the wounded man. Then Nikolaos dipped the strips of cloth in the steaming pot Livilla held, wrapped the leaves and flowers in the moist cloth, and pressed the poultice against the man's wound.

Everyone turned as a piercing cry came from the villa. A figure ran towards the barn, crying and shouting, "Emilio! Emilio!" Argolicus realized it was the young woman with the large brown eyes who had served them in the atrium. She fell sobbing on the straw next to the young man and took his hand. He took the willow stick out of his mouth, looked up, smiled, and said, "Dacia."

They looked into each other's eyes. Argolicus watched Emilio's body relax as love, a stronger soporific than the pain reducing white willow, took over his body.

Tatius broke the spell. "Dacia," he said in a soft, but commanding, voice, "that's enough. Emilio will rest. Go back to the house with my mother." The unspoken command to Livilla was clear enough. She handed the bowl to Dacia, and they both walked back toward the villa.

Emilio looked up from the straw at Tatius. "Thank you, Master," he said. Then he put the willow back in his mouth and closed his eyes. Tatius nodded, gave Pup a quick command, and headed off to the orchard with the three slaves.

"Well," Secundus sighed, "that was an unusual occurrence. Let's go in for the meal. Tatius will be in shortly. And those two, Emilio and Dacia, they were so much trouble before my father died."

"Why?" Argolicus asked. "They looked so full of love. Did you see how his body relaxed when she arrived?"

"That was the problem. Dacia is a servant, Emilio is a slave. He asked my father to allow them a formal *conjunctio* which slaves do all the time at the big ecclesiastical estates and large landowner estates."

Argolicus nodded his head. As far as Secundus was concerned, he, himself, would be one of those large landowners.

"But Father forbade it," Secundus continued. "As I said, he was arbitrarily controlling. There was no reason for them not to marry in the slave's manner and as long as she, a free *rustico,* wanted to join with him, they could be married."

The dynamics of lower social class life suddenly struck Argolicus. He thought of the formality of his *consortium* with Julia. The family arrangement, in which he and Julia had little to say, the crowd of guests at the ceremony, and a marriage of kindness, but without the love he had seen in those two young people's eyes.

"What was his reason?" Argolicus asked.

"Reason! Ha," Secundus snorted. "Father didn't need a reason. He liked to manipulate people, just for the power. Of course, soon after Father died, Emilio asked Tatius, and he agreed. So, as soon as the formal mourning period is over they will be married. Among the servants and slaves here, their love is celebrated because they overcame the obstacle to their union and that a *rustico* woman would marry a slave. It does have quite a romantic ring to it, don't you think?"

"Love is a powerful force, I've heard," Argolicus answered.

Secundus gave him a querying look, but Argolicus didn't respond.

"Well, then," Secundus said as he gestured toward the villa, "let's go eat. I know you have dinner parties in the evening, but here at this small farm we eat at mid-day."

"I'll speak with my tutor for a minute." Argolicus turned back toward Emilio and Nikolaos.

Secundus waited at the barn door. Nikolaos rose.

"How is he?" Argolicus asked.

"Master, it will take a while to heal up. It is a deep puncture, but there were no splinters or other objects to cause festering. I think he will be fine in time."

"Nikolaos, is it possible that the father could have been poisoned? You were there. You heard the widow Livilla describe his death. Could we be looking at more than a widow being sent away after her husband's death?"

Nikolaos pondered, then answered, "With all those herbs in the garden and the others by the creek, yes. It is possible. But who would do such a thing?" Then, as soon as he said it, a light came into his eyes. He glanced at Emilio.

"Yes," Argolicus said nodding. "I thought as much. I think we will spend the day here, following their farm schedule, a meal, a time of rest, and then work. But our work will be observing, questioning, and thinking. I'm going in."

"I'll stay here with him for a while," Nikolaos said as Emilio groaned.

Argolicus met Secundus at the door, and they walked into the burning sunlight.

❁   3   ❁

MERIDIATIO

Argolicus ate with the family in the garden under the plane tree on simple stools set around a table. Dacia served with watery eyes, distracted by the injured Emilio in the barn. The meal was simple but ample: olives, hard cooked eggs, beans, and braised white fish with herbs.

Livilla turned her simpering face toward Argolicus, "Would you care for more wine?" Then without waiting for an answer she called, "Dacia, more wine."

"Thank you. I'm quite satisfied. This is a filling meal. You are a good cook, Livilla."

"Oh, I don't cook." She waved her hand in a girlish gesture. "The servants prepare the food. I suggest the menus based on what we have on hand. And, the boys make sure we have plenty." She beamed at Tatius and Secundus.

Dacia poured wine for everyone.

"So, Mother, were your questions answered?" Tatius asked, glancing at Argolicus.

Livilla lost her flirtatious look and for a second she looked somber. Then she turned to Argolicus while speaking to Tatius,

"Yes. My questions were answered. I am most grateful, Your Sublimity."

"Good," Tatius said. He turned to Argolicus. "After siesta, I will show you around the grounds. Rumor has it you are studying forms of agriculture. Is that right? I can show you what we do here. We may be small, but our produce is excellent."

Argolicus was startled, and then realized there must be many rumors floating around about the local who had made it big in Rome and then returned home. And, he was taken off guard; he had planned to return home after siesta. Then he thought about the heat that flourished outside of the great tree's shade and decided returning in the evening was a good idea. "I would like that," he replied.

"My office has a soft couch. You can rest there. I'm sure you are accustomed to reading, but we have no books, only ledgers."

"Thank you, Tatius. First I'll check with my tutor to see how the herbs are working."

After the meal, Livilla disappeared in her room. Tatius went off with Pup. Secundus said he would look at the ledgers. Argolicus wanted to check on the situation in the barn. He noticed that none of the family seemed to be interested. Dacia started clearing the table.

When Argolicus arrived in the barn and its cooling shade, he was surprised to see another man hunkered over Emilio, chatting in whispers with Nikolaos. In spite of the rough condition of his clothes, the most remarkable thing about him was his weathered face. At first, Argolicus took him for an old man, but as he drew closer, he realized that his browned skin and crow's feet were the result of living out of doors. His tunic was made of rough, unbleached linen wrinkled and stained with wear. The shoulders of the garment had seen so much sunlight the rough flax was bleached to cream.

Argolicus took off his hat and wiped his forehead grateful for the thick walls and roof of the barn. The animals were all sleeping quietly. The only sound was the two men whispering and an occasional murmur from Emilio.

The man glanced up and stopped talking. Nikolaos turned. "Master, Emilio is resting. I just changed the dressing and see no red swelling." He glanced at the other man who was eying Argolicus warily. "This is Bene, Dacia's father."

"Bene, greetings," Argolicus said.

"Your Sublimity," Bene answered with an almost imperceptible mock.

"Are you *the* Bene?"

"I am."

"I didn't believe you were real. The Bene of local legend? So many stories of your..." Argolicus paused briefly for a word, "your actions."

Bene smiled. "Most of them are true, all except for commandeering the ship and sailing it to Hispania."

Argolicus felt the connections came together inside his head. Secundus had mentioned that the girl was a *rustica*. They were the poorest Romans: unlanded, working at odd jobs when they could find them, living in the hills or wherever they could without a shelter. Some of them, without work, were outlaws--thieves and bandits. Here in southern Italy, there were no large cities, so the *rustico* population was large. The church, which collected taxes for the cities and seemed to skim off large amounts, provided work for some. Landowners had a demand for more. And small farms like the family here had work for one or two.

Bene was infamous for his brash deeds. He was revered like a saint by the poor--*rustico* and slave--because he pillaged the rich and distributed food, money, and clothing to the needy.

Bene spoke, bringing Argolicus back to the moment. "Emilio is a good lad. He treats Dacia with kindness. But that's not all, he respects her. They listen to each other. I've rarely seen such devotion, admiration, and...love between two people. My daughter is fortunate." He reached out and gently touch Emilio's head.

"Master," Nikolaos said. "He has been telling me how Valerius treated his servants, like Dacia."

Emilio opened his eyes, bit down on the willow twig, removed it from his mouth, and spoke. "I hated him. The way he treated Dacia. It wasn't that he hit her. He took every opportunity to humiliate her with words. He made her do...things."

"When I found out," Bene said, "I wanted to punish him. I was thinking of a plan to steal the peaches, and then...he died. Nobody misses him. Not even his family."

"Stealing peaches," Emilio scoffed. "I had another plan, but Dacia wouldn't agree."

"Another plan?" Argolicus asked.

"Yes, out there in that garden. Poisonous plants." Emilio shifted his weight, trying to get his leg in a comfortable position. "I thought if we could..."

"Well, you didn't," Bene interrupted. "How could you even think of asking Dacia to do such a terrible thing? Murder is not the way."

"That's what Dacia said. But I hated him." Emilio pounded his fist in the straw, emphasizing his emotion.

"They were right. For a slave like you, it would be instant death. For a girl like Dacia there would not be much justice. Our governor, Venantius, is under orders from the king to quell any rebellion." Argolicus glanced at Bene.

"Venantius!" Bene spat. "How much more corrupt could anyone be. He outshines the church in his venal activities. Dacia would probably be given to his bodyguards as a toy before being executed." He gazed into the middle distance. "I raised her. She has values, and she lives by them."

Argolicus realized that Dacia had every reason to want to kill Valerius; his belittling attitude and sexual predation were nothing compared to his prevention of her marriage.

"I will speak to her," Argolicus said. "Yes, Venantius, and as others..."

Bene interrupted him. "And the ecclesiastical holdings. They trade people and buy children of poor people who have no way to live. The nature of Christ doesn't matter whether it is one God, or three, or even the God and Son that you believe." He gave Argolicus a challenging stare.

Argolicus was taken aback with how much this wild stranger knew about him.

Bene continued, "Have you heard how the monks up north tried to poison the pious Benedictus? His following grows as he speaks of an ordered and peaceful life. How can we have an ordered and peaceful life when these outrages continue? Strange that we would have the same name when our ways of dealing with corruption are so different. I believe in direct help. He believes in spiritual peace."

Argolicus wondered if the fiery temperament could lead Bene to kill. Murder was different than robbing and distributing to the poor. And the way he spoke of Dacia and her upbringing. He found killing someone else unlikely.

"Well, he's dead now," Emilio interjected, bringing everyone back to Valerius and his death. "May his soul burn forever."

"Emilio," Argolicus asked, "who else would want him dead?"

"Who else? Everyone. Tatius wanted the farm. Secundus suffered under his scathing remarks. His wife. The workers in the house. The workers on the farm. Everyone. He was an autocrat and cruel just to be cruel."

"Many men are generally disliked, but that doesn't mean they are killed. Perhaps it was just a thought that makes no sense and he died of apoplexy." Argolicus said, thinking he had said too much to a slave and a wild man who was known criminal.

Bene reached out and touched Emilio's arm. "I must go. You seem to be in good hands. I'll say goodbye to Dacia and leave this place. I'll see you soon." He turned toward the door.

"Thank you for coming," Emilio said. "It means a lot to me. I will be well. Nikolaos here says the healing will take time but that

I will recover." He smiled up at Bene who was adjusting a dagger under his sleeve. "Don't get caught with that dagger."

Bene laughed and left the barn.

"Master," Nikolaos said. "Let us leave Emilio so he can rest. Sleeping is a good cure for wounds." He turned to Emilio, "Is it better? Do you think you can sleep for a while?"

Emilio nodded and closed his eyes, fatigued from the fall, the wound, and the conversation with Bene.

Nikolaos stood and nodded to Argolicus.

Argolicus bent over Emilio, "Nikolaos is skilled with herbs and healing. If he says you will recover, you will."

Emilio's eyes fluttered open. "Thank you. And thank you for not raising an alarm about Bene. Underneath his gruff ways, he is a good man. He is dedicated to helping." He shut his eyes again.

Argolicus and Nikolaos found the study and quietly sat in chairs by a large table covered with receipts, notes, and ledgers.

"Will he recover?" Argolicus asked.

"Oh, yes. The widow Valerius knows about herbs. I took notes on her garden. She has many herbs but the calendula and symphytum should help the healing and keep the wound from swelling and infection. She told me she has been working with the plants since she first came here. It was the one domain that was hers. Valerius never bothered with the herbs."

"Do you think that my speculation was just a fantasy?" Argolicus asked.

"Well, poisoning didn't seem to occur to anyone in the family. No one brought it up as an alternative. Apoplexy is common in men who become angry easily."

"Yes, but if one of the family had poisoned him, they certainly wouldn't bring it up as a possibility. You heard how she described his death. He wasn't particularly angry at the time. They were sitting in the garden after an evening supper. It just seemed to come without any strong emotions from him."

"Master, that is true. But, sometimes the body just gets tired and ends."

"What about the girl? She must have hated him. She serves the food. She could easily have put something in his food."

Nikolaos was silent for a moment. "Let me go talk to her. I'll ask for some food since I missed the meal."

SLAVE AND RUSTICA

The heat from the kitchen fires made the room almost unbearable, and the open door and windows only let in the heat from the from the midday sun. Dacia and a boy of about thirteen were putting away dishes and pots when Nikolaos entered.

"Ah, the healer," Dacia said, giving him a large smile. "Have you come for some food? You are more than welcome. I am so grateful you helped Emilio. Without you, he would have lain suffering with no attention or treatment." She took the bowl in her hand, opened a cupboard in the pantry and began filling the bowl with leftovers from the meal.

"Left with no treatment?" Nikolaos asked. "What about the widow? Wouldn't she help him? She knows the herbs."

"Oh, she knows the herbs, that is certain. But, her generosity does not reach outside the household to the farm workers. I'm sure she helped you because she wants to impress your master."

"My, master?" Nikolaos was perplexed.

"Ha, I thought you were smart with learning. Yes, your master. She's about to be put out into the world. She is looking for a man. Look at your master. Tall, handsome, rich, respected, knowledgeable. Everything her husband was not. Why wouldn't she want to impress him? Any woman would want your master. I like his blond curls." She lit her face with a big broad grin.

Nikolaos hadn't thought about that. It was true, all of that, and more. The widow would be desperate for someone now that her stepsons wanted her gone.

"You're his tutor, educated, well-read. And every tutor is an advisor. You should let him know," Dacia said. She handed him the bowl and motioned toward the large table in the center of the kitchen.

Nikolaos sat on a stool and began to eat. "This is good. Thank you."

"On the farm we have food. It's one of the few things we do have. Look around. Did you see any books, or carved furniture, or elegant plates? Food is what we have. Look at people like my father, they have nothing. This household is rich in the eyes of people like him. And, for me, before I started working here. Plus I found Emilio here."

"How did you two meet? He's a farm slave. He lives in a different building. He doesn't come in the villa."

Dacia's brown eyes lit up. She smiled. She flicked back a dark lock from her cheek. "I was putting out the laundry to dry. He was at the corral getting ready to take the sheep out to graze. It was his turn." Her eyes looked into the middle distance as she remembered and the corners of her full lips turned up. "He smiled. That was all it took." Her lips parted in a full-blown smile at the memory.

Nikolaos finished his last bite of food and handed the dish to Dacia. She took it and washed the dish and the implements. He noticed she kept a clean and orderly kitchen. Just as she quickly cleaned his dishes, everything was organized in the food preparation area.

Dacia continued, "Emilio told me he felt the same way. The

moment he saw me..." She paused and blushed. "He...we...it was the beginning," she said and came to a halt.

Nikolaos smiled, and said, "Emilio told me there was a problem with Valerius."

As quickly as she had smiled before, Dacia frowned, and her face clouded. Her dark lashes came down over her eyes as she looked down at the table. "He wanted me," she murmured. The blush had faded from her cheeks, and she looked pale. Still looking at the table, she said, "He..."

"Bene told us," Nikolaos prompted.

"Ah, my father. In many ways he is noble. He says he hates the noblemen and the rich ecclesiastics, but it is theoretical hate. The feeling I had for Valerius burned in my heart. I wanted him dead. I did. I watched him from the doorway as he clutched his chest in the garden."

Nikolaos asked, "He did? He clutched his chest?"

Dacia looked up from the table, "Yes. He grabbed at his tunic. He kept saying, 'I can't stop it. I can't stop it.' He rolled on the ground. He looked up and saw me watching from the doorway. I think he thought I had poisoned him. He gave me one accusatory look before the spasms took his body. It didn't take him long to die."

She stopped and looked directly at Nikolaos.

"It was a horrible death. There was nothing peaceful about it. He was in agony. I was repulsed, but I was relieved. No more grabbing me in corners. No more of his hot breath in my face or his rough hands tugging at my clothes." Tears started from the corners of her eyes.

Nikolaos reached out his hand, "Dacia, he is gone now."

She nodded silently as the tears streamed down her face.

"Why am I crying?" she asked. "I hated him. He used me. His wife pretended she didn't notice. I don't like her much, either."

Nikolaos nodded. "My master keeps a strict but open house-hold. I've known him since he was a boy. But, when we were in

Rome, things like this happened all the time. I'd be in the kitchen eating and hearing stories of abuse and torment, much worse than yours. Couples like you and Emilio are deliberately separated, and one is sold away. Whippings for no reason. You may think that Valerius was cruel, and he was, but he was not as evil as you think."

"When it is happening to you, it feels like the worst thing in the world," Dacia said.

Nikolaos nodded. "That is always true, for everyone. I wasn't born a slave." He left it at that. "Why would Valerius think you had poisoned him? Why did he give you that look? Wasn't it just apoplexy?"

"I hadn't thought about that," Dacia said. She thought about her answer. "I thought it was apoplexy at the time. I thought it was his one last mean gesture. Everyone said it was apoplexy. When he was angry, his face would get red. Sometimes it looked as though his eyes would pop out."

"Yes, that happens. It is typical," Nikolaos said.

"But, now that I think about it, he wasn't angry. They were just sitting in the garden talking quietly." She closed her eyes remembering the scene. "I was coming out to clear away the last dishes. He clutched his chest, and it started. I don't know how it happened."

Nikolaos was ready to leave. "Dacia, this conversation has upset you. I hope you won't think I've pried too deeply, bringing up unpleasant memories."

"The memories will always be there," Dacia said. "But now, Emilio and I will be married. No one will get in the way of our happiness. Now that Tatius is in charge things run according to order, but he is not mean. Look out the window," she said, gesturing toward the open window and the door. "It is beautiful here, and peaceful. The turmoil of the cities that Bene relates...it doesn't happen here. Plus, Bene told me he is saving to buy freedom for Emilio. If that happens, I don't see us leaving, just living here and contributing to the farm. We have no grand ambitions. I leave that to my father." She smiled as Nikolaos got up from the table.

"Thank you, Dacia. The meal was delicious. Emilio will hurt for a while, and he will have a scar, but he will heal and be back to working soon."

"Thank you, Nikolaos, for your presence of mind and your help. Even though my mistress knows her plants, she doesn't share freely with the slaves. All of us are left to fend for ourselves. Tatius gives us time to heal, but he doesn't know the herbs."

"You are welcome." Nikolaos turned from her grateful dark eyes and returned to the study.

Argolicus sat in a chair with his head bowed. He was thinking how someone like Bene could give long speeches about theory and how he, himself, could think the long thoughts but few words came out. He lifted his head when Nikolaos entered. "Anything?"

"Good food, but nothing that we didn't know. Emilio..."

"Yes, Emilio. I've been sitting here thinking while you were gone. Bene is motivated by fatherly care, but I don't see him as a killer. And he didn't have an opportunity."

"And after my talk with Dacia, I don't see her taking action. She certainly had reason to hate Valerius."

"Mmmmm. The brothers. Especially Tatius. He seems so bent on controlling the farm, to the extent that he wants to displace his mother, even if she is a step-mother."

"The thing is," Nikolaos said, "we don't know Valerius was killed. It could all have happened just as the widow described. Maybe we are looking for something that isn't there."

They sat in silence, drinking in the cool air of the quiet study until a discreet knock at the door interrupted their thoughts.

❈ 5 ❈

BROTHERLY SUSPICION

Secundus slipped through the door. "Your Sublimity." He bit his lip and then blurted out in one breath, "I've been thinking about what you said."

Argolicus looked up, raised an eyebrow, and said, "Yes."

Secundus glanced at Nikolaos and then looked at Argolicus with his plain face slightly flushed. "You started me thinking. Why would Tatius want to disinherit me? I've been so caught up in brotherly rivalry, something that has existed since we were small, that I hadn't thought about the reason why. He's always played the older brother role. He's not a bully like our father was, but he puts himself in charge."

Argolicus nodded.

Secundus scraped a hand through his thick brown hair. "When you asked the question, we were interrupted by the commotion with the slave falling, but I started thinking about it. Not as an angry younger brother, but looking at the reason behind his reason."

Nikolaos quietly drew out his tablet.

Argolicus asked, "What did you discover...when you thought about it?"

Secundus pulled a second chair close to Argolicus and sat. "He's greedy. His decision has little to do with me as a brother. Obviously, family ties aren't important to him. But, that's why it doesn't make any sense." He bit his lip and stood up. He went to the study's small window and gazed out. "Without me, the business part would fall apart," he said staring out at the valley. "Your question caused me to re-evaluate what I do and how I keep us in touch with buyers and shippers."

Argolicus nodded again then asked, "What would happen if you went away?"

Secundus rubbed the back of his neck as he thought. Then he walked back over to the chair and sat.

"I hadn't thought about that. You are helping me think about the consequences of Tatius' demands. I would have no trouble finding work. People know me." He let out an audible breath and looked directly at Argolicus.

"Why...I could...it would be possible...I could set up my own business for other produce farmers. I would do for many what I do for just one." His flushed face returned to normal, his eyes gleamed, and he smiled. "I already have contacts. I could charge a small fee. I already know many farmers I could help." He slapped his knees and stood up again.

"What a good idea. You have helped me see this from an entirely different point of view. I could bring Mother with me. This is splendid. Just splendid."

"You would take your mother with you?" Argolicus asked, thinking his mother had been wrong that both sons wanted her gone.

"Oh, yes. She is the only mother I have known. Tatius wants to throw her out into the world. His desire for control overrides everything. The slaves and servants consider him fair, and for them he is, but for his family..." Secundus hesitated for a moment, fingering accounts sheets on the table. "He doesn't think about people as people. He thinks it would all be easier if he had complete control."

"But, losing you would harm the farm's prosperity. It doesn't make sense," Argolicus countered.

"Tatius doesn't think. He does."

"Ah," Argolicus said. "I've known others like that. I've seen it happen. They take action and then find themselves cornered without a way out."

"Yes, exactly. That's what it feels like he is doing. Sometimes I think…" Secundus stopped and rubbed the top of his thighs. "Ah, you see, I am just the other way. My mind can build possibilities that are not true."

"What do you mean?" Argolicus asked.

"Well, sometimes I think…I think…It's to awful to say out loud." He sent a pleading look at Argolicus.

"You have unfounded suspicions?" Argolicus said raising an eyebrow.

Secundus looked him in the eye and then looked down at his hands resting on his knees. "Yes, suspicions. But they are ungrounded. There's nothing…"

Argolicus waited, knowing it was the best way to keep someone talking. Nikolaos wrote something on his tablet.

Secundus scratched the back of his neck and stared at the accounts stacked up on the table. "Let me put it another way. I think that Father's dying saved us from more grief."

Argolicus nodded again and asked, "You think that if he had not died…"

"Yes, if he had not died, I think Tatius would have hastened his death…somehow. Perhaps an accident out in the fields or…" He paused again, looking at Argolicus, hoping he would verbalize what he, himself, could not say.

But, Argolicus remained silent countering Secundus' pleading look with a questioning gaze.

Secundus reached to a far corner of the table for a stack of notes. He picked them up and repositioned the stack in front of him on the table. Then he picked up the stack and waved them in the air.

"You see, he has another trade venture that is proving quite lucrative." He waved the stack about again. "I keep the accounts. But...Father didn't approve. He felt Tatius would eventually destroy the good name of our family."

"What do you mean?" Argolicus was now curious.

Secundus gestured toward the window. "Up there. Up in the hills, he has another venture." He brought his hand down to his lap. "He makes *garum*. Well, it's not *garum*."

Argolicus furrowed his brow.

Secundus frowned. "But it's not *garum*. I really didn't like this idea, except...except...It is making money. More money than the farm. I keep the accounts." He waved the sheets around in the air again.

"I don't understand," Argolicus said, his frown deepening. "How can it be *garum*, but not *garum*? And why is it in the hills? I thought *garum* factories were close to fishing ports."

"Well, that's just it," Secundus continued. "Pure *garum* is made from mackerel, and the best from only mackerel. The second is a mixture of fish and anchovy. Have you been down to the fisherman's port? They lay out the fish so buyers can buy the best parts. But Tatius does the opposite."

Nikolaos stopped scratching on his pad and turned his full attention to Secundus.

Argolicus sighed. "I have heard of this. I have a friend, Ebrimuth. Tell me."

"Tatius hired a man from Squillace. That man goes to the fish market and buys the leftover fish and fish parts. He loads them up on a cart and drives up to the hill. We've a...Tatius has a factory there. Well, it's a big kitchen."

"A kitchen?" Argolicus was now intrigued. "*Garum* ferments in the sun for months. What happens in the kitchen?"

"This fellow, his name is Amon. He's from Egypt or some place in Africa. Amon takes the fish parts up to the kitchen. There are a few slaves there. They add salt and cook the fish. It's a horrible stink. That's why they've hidden it up in the hills. They cook the salted fish parts down, pour the liquid through a sieve. They pour that liquid into fancy urns and sell it at premium prices to their market."

"Who would buy this stuff?" Argolicus asked, perplexed. "Any good Roman would know this stuff didn't taste right."

"That's just it. You answered your own question. Any good Roman would know." Secundus tried to smile, but it was more of a grimace. His neck and cheeks flushed. "You know how up north the Romans of Italy try to mimic King Theoderic's court? They've forsaken togas, dress in silks, practice Greek, and mimic the king's people in court. But all over Italy the People, especially near Rome and in the South, try to imitate the Roman ways. They want to be part of Italy now that they live here."

"Yes, yes. Explain, Secundus." A germinal suspicion entered his mind.

Secundus swallowed. "Tatius sells this imitation *garum* to the People. You know, the king's people. They come from far away to the North and East. They are barbarians." He looked guiltily at Argolicus, tried another smile with no success. "They don't know the difference."

Argolicus shot up from his chair in anger. "I'm losing patience with this family. Your mother and her flirtatious ways. Your brother and his sneaky business. And you. You keep the accounts for this business. My mother, the mother who sent me here to help your mother, is one of the People. That makes *me* one of the people you are defrauding, too. Because of my father you think of my recent role in Rome, but I am a true mixture of the two races."

Secundus looked as though he would grovel on the floor. Instead of looking Argolicus in the eye, he stared at the account sheets in his hand. "I know. We know. Everyone knows. Your family, your mother. Your meteoric rise in Rome. Cassiodorus. Even here on this small farm, we know about the big families around us." He swallowed again. "But we also hear that you are fair. That you are...wise. And that you go out of your way to help people. Your entire household is known. Your tutor helped Emilio today. That's why I was hesitant to tell you."

Argolicus' voice grew firm in cold rage. "I will report this dishonest practice. This family will deal with Venantius, and I will be done with all of you."

"Master, Venantius?" Nikolaos exclaimed.

"Yes, I have no authority. Venantius is the governor. They can exchange venal practices."

"Your Sublimity," Secundus whined. "Is there a way to stop this? Venantius will ask for more money than we have."

"That is your dilemma. Where is Tatius? I will see this kitchen factory for myself." He strode to the door and opened it. Livilla and Tatius were standing in the hallway, their faces the epitome of dismay. Pup sat by his master's knee.

Livilla looked at Tatius, "How could you? Why didn't you tell me?" She stood quietly crying.

Secundus rushed to her side.

"I am an honest farmer and a good businessman," Tatius stated emphatically. "There is no reason to tell Venantius."

"There is," Argolicus growled. "Take me to this kitchen."

UPHILL AND DOWN

rgolicus felt as if his skin were burning. After the cool of the study, the outside heat seemed like stepping into a furnace. With Nikolaos, he trudged up the hill behind the villa with Secundus, Tatius, and a slave who carried two large skins full of water. Pup seemed unaffected by the heat. The big dog raced ahead and ran back. Then he raced over to the creek and back again as they plodded up in the heat. The warm air carried the scent of dry grass in the sun.

Everyone was silent. Argolicus trudged uphill. He heard the water sloshing in the skins the slave toted over his shoulder. He heard Pup splashing in the creek. He thought about his rash outbreak with Tatius. He had put himself in an uncomfortable position. Now he had to walk up the hill in the blazing heat, inspect the kitchen, and make a decision. Yes, he would make a decision after he had seen the factory.

Secundus broke the silence. "Perhaps you could reconsider, Your Sublimity. We barely make a living here without the kitchen. We have eager buyers, and right now we can't produce enough. The People here are far from the fineries of Ravenna. We supply a need."

Argolicus thought about not replying. Yes, he was still angry. But he relented. "I'll see the kitchen and then make a decision."

"Your Sublimity, you will see that we make a fine *liquamen*."

"Fine?"

"Well, um, we have a fast but pure process."

"Pure, but using the cheapest ingredients," Argolicus corrected. "Not fine. Not *garum*. Not expensive. You are cheating your buyers."

Secundus couldn't keep his face from reddening and went back to silence after his failed attempt at conciliation.

The dry grass grew thinner as they climbed. The trail disappeared among small rocks. Each step required careful placement on the uneven surface. The rocks had absorbed the heat from the sun, and their warmth radiated through Argolicus' sandals as they climbed. The oily smell of cooking fish replaced the fresh scent of dry grass. Argolicus decided this was one of the more unpleasant walks of his life. Cheating men, uncomfortable silence, hot sun, rough rocks, and the rank odor of fish all contributed to his unease.

With Tatius leading the way they topped the hill crest. Below was a small valley with several buildings. Men moved in lethargy from the heat among the buildings. Two horses napped, tethered in a small shed protected from the burning sun. A four-wheeled cart stood next to the shed baking in the sunlight. The surrounding rocky hills formed a bowl which trapped the fetid air. The odor of fish was overwhelming.

A tall, slender man emerged from one of the structures. "Tatius," he called.

Tatius waved before they descended the uneven rocks to the kitchen. When they reached the valley floor, Tatius said, "Amon, this is *vir nobilis*, Gaius Vitellius Argolicus. He has come to inspect the kitchens."

Amon's dark eyes in his olive-skinned face flashed a brief question as he bowed slightly to Argolicus. "Your Sublimity, allow me to show you the process."

Tatius nodded. "We'll have some water first." He gestured to the slave who had lugged the water skins up the hill. Amon disappeared and returned with drinking bowls. Argolicus realized he was extremely thirsty. He took a proffered bowl and drank deeply. He handed the bowl to the slave.

"Thank you," he said. The slave nodded gravely.

Amon gestured toward the horses and the cart. "We bring the fish up from the market. In here," he gestured to a large shed. The roof of the large structure covered various work areas. Some had tables and baskets, others had more baskets and stacks of urns, while the actual kitchen was in the center where numerous clay stoves held large cooking pots with utensils lined along the sides. In the nearest quarter, slaves pounded away in mortars.

Argolicus felt queasy, and the kitchen seemed to rock. The odor of fish was overpowering inside the shed.

"We mash all the fish parts into a lumpy paste," Ammon said gesturing toward the busy slaves. He led them among the work areas. "Then we take the mashed fish into the kitchen." He led them forward to the center workspace of multiple fire stoves. "We cook in the early morning. We mix the mashed fish with salt and water and cook until the mixture is thick. This valley is like a natural bowl, we have our own water supply from the well over there." He pointed to layered bricks covered with a board. "You notice, Your Sublimity, the kitchen is quite clean and organized."

Argolicus nodded. Everything was clean. The utensils had been cleaned and were set out neatly next to the fire pits. His head felt light. He felt as though he could drink another three bowls of water. He felt lightheaded.

"In here," Amon continued as they walked to another area of the work shed filled with woven baskets and large bowls, "The cooked mash is strained." He reached a work table covered with basket strainers. He picked up two strainers. "First, we strain the liquid for large parts." He held up one basket woven loosely with wide strips. "Then we strain again and again." He held up the second basket which was finely woven.

"The liquid that comes out of the final straining," Amon said, waving the finely woven basket, " is stored in these urns." He gestured to lines of urns stacked nearby. "Twice a week we pour the liquid into small vials which I take to market. We have one main stall at the market in town and..."

Argolicus reached to support himself on one of the clay stoves but collapsed to the ground instead.

⁂

When Argolicus opened his eyes, the first thing he saw was Pup's giant dark eyes gazing down at him as Nikolaos wiped his forehead with a damp cloth. The giant white dog lowered his head and licked Argolicus' damp face. The dog's tongue lapping at his eyelids encouraged him to sit up.

Tatius, Secundus, and Amon stood in a circle around him. Tatius looked annoyed. Secundus scowled in worry. Amon said, "The northerners have trouble with the heat. It is the fair skin."

The slave offered Argolicus a bowl of water which he took gratefully. The water seemed to cool his entire body as it trickled down his throat.

"Drink slowly, Master," Nikolaos said as the slave poured fresh water on the cloth. Nikolaos squeezed the cloth over Argolicus' head and then pressed the damp cloth against his neck.

Argolicus looked up at the concerned faces. "Amon is right. But I haven't had that happen since I was a boy."

Pup started licking his neck, and then his cheek again. Argolicus smiled. "I believe Pup is concerned about my well-being."

There was silence, and then everyone laughed. Argolicus set the bowl on the ground and Pup lapped up the last drops of water.

He reached over to pat the great dog's broad head. Pup licked his wrist.

Argolicus struggled to his feet as Nikolaos pressed the cool, damp cloth against his other wrist. Argolicus pushed the cloth away. "That's enough, Nikolaos. You and Pup have restored me."

Pup's tail began thumping against the side of the clay stove at the mention of his name.

Argolicus looked around the kitchen at the stacks of baskets, the neatly ordered utensils, and the clean work surfaces. "I have an idea that will keep us all from dealing with Venantius."

Tatius looked relieved. Secundus blurted, "What is it?"

Argolicus stooped to retrieve the hat that had fallen to the ground when he fainted, but Nikolaos scooped it up before he could reach it. He held the cloth out again for the slave to pour more water. He squeezed the cloth gently and then folded it into a square. He placed the damp cloth on Argolicus' head and then placed the hat over the cloth. "There," he said. "Remember when you did that as a boy?"

Argolicus remembered, appreciating his tutor's help, and smiled at Nikolaos. "Venantius," he said. "Now that I have seen your kitchen, I have a solution that will work."

Tatius stood silent. Secundus fiddled with the neck of his tunic. Amon nodded.

"The kitchen is clean and well-ordered. Your process is authentic—but not for *garum*."

The three anxious men shuffled.

"You have the traditional method for making *liquamen*. Your ingredients are certainly substandard."

More anxious shuffling from Tatius, Secundus, and Amon.

"If you sell your product as *liquamen* and certainly at a reduced price, I see no reason to involve the Governor."

Tatius closed his eyes and shook his head in relief. "Your Sublimity, you decision is more than I could have asked."

Argolicus said, "*Liquamen*. Low-grade *liquamen*. At a reduced price."

"*Liquamen* at a reduced price," Tatius repeated.

"Perhaps we can invest in a *garum* plant near the sea, without transportation costs," Secundus said, thinking out loud.

"Perhaps," Tatius said.

"Mother will be relieved to hear the news. Let's go back and tell her," Secundus said. "With your permission, Your Sublimity?"

"Yes, then I will take my leave," Argolicus answered, glad he had somehow made it easier for his mother's acquaintance.

"The walk back is downhill, Your Sublimity. It will be easier."

They left the kitchen and instead of following the trail, headed down the cart path. "We'll cut over toward the farm when the cart track nears the creek," Tatius said.

Unlike the silent journey up the hill, the walk back was filled with chatter, mostly from Secundus, about business plans, new distribution for the *liquamen*, where he could find a suitable site to start a *garum* factory, what percentage of their earnings would go into the factory, and the like. A chatter filled with hopes and dreams full of the young man's indomitable spirit of enterprise. Every once in a while, Tatius would grunt assent or answer a question.

"We'll cut over here," Tatius said as they reached a small grove of oak trees, casting shade over the grassy slope. They were below the rock-strewn top and back on the sloping fields. The air once again filled with the scent of grass in the summer sun. Argolicus could hear the water in the creek as they headed for the willows and bushes that grew along the creek bank. Pup rushed ahead, did some furious lapping and splashing in the water, then came bounding back. He stood by Tatius and shook himself, sending water droplets in a fine spray onto everyone's legs.

"Good boy," Tatius said patting him on the head, the first kind gesture Argolicus had seen him give the big white dog.

They all took off their sandals to wade across the creek. The cool water was a welcome relief to Argolicus. The scent of willows and rose-laurel and the water of the creek revived his spirits. As he sat on the ground on the other side of the creek to fasten his sandals, he felt completely restored. He could hear Pup splashing around farther down the creek. Then he heard the big dog crashing and snapping sticks in the shrubs.

Tatius led them to the path they had used earlier in the afternoon to go up to the kitchen and headed down toward the farm.

Secundus continued with his dreamy chatter. "We already have the distribution network. It won't be that hard. Some people will grumble at the change, but it won't be that hard. We'll increase volume and even though our prices will be lower we will still make a handsome profit."

Tatius grunted.

"I'm sure with our connections it won't be hard to find a place to set up the *garum*..."

Pup came up the hill from the creek proudly carrying a stick with a few long, thin leaves dangling. He plopped down on the ground and began to chew vigorously, making contented grunts as the stick cracked in his teeth.

"Secundus," Tatius said. "We have time to work this all out. It would be best, right now, to thank his Sublimity for his leniency."

Secundus reddened and looked at Argolicus. "Your Sublimity, thank you for reconsidering our production. I—we—I mean, Tatius and I are grateful for your solution. Your reputation is validated. You are wise and fair. We are grateful—"

"*Liquamen*, reduced prices," Argolicus said. "That is what it is. Just call it that, charge fair prices for an inferior product, and we'll let the matter rest."

Pup started whining and then let out a pitiful moan. They all turned toward the dog, lying on the ground, the stick between his paws, his eyes pleading as he let out another moan, writhed on the grass, and dropped his head to the ground.

❧ 7 ❧

DOGBANE

"Pup!" Tatius ran down the slope and knelt by the big white dog. Secundus and Nikolaos followed behind. Tatius leaned down and put his head against the great dog's chest. "No! No, no, no."

Argolicus quickly finished with his sandals and ran down to the dog.

Nikolaos touched Tatius on the shoulder. "I can try something. I saw this before."

Tatius looked up at the tutor and silently nodded his head. Tears streamed down the taciturn farmer's cheeks.

Nikolaos ran to the nearest willow on the creek bank and broke off a branch. He returned and knelt by the dog's head. "This will be unpleasant," he said, warning Tatius.

Tatius nodded again.

Nikolaos put his hands on Pup's jaws to open his mouth wide. He took the willow stick and forced it past the teeth down into the limp dog's throat. Nothing happened, and Nikolaos tried to hide his disappointment. Suddenly, the dog convulsed and retched. As Nikolaos pulled the willow stick out green foam and pieces of chewed stick splattered on the ground. Pup retched again, and more pieces sprayed onto the ground. The big dog opened his eyes and looked up at Nikolaos, turned to look at Tatius.

"Pup," the big man said. The dog gave a feeble tail wag.

"Now we must give him sweets. Peach juice is sweet. We'll try that," Nikolaos said.

Tatius lifted Pup gently, placing his arms under the dog's forelegs. He raised the dog over his head a draped the big body around his neck. "It's not that far," he said, as he started down the hill carrying the big dog.

❧

Nikolaos ran ahead, while the group followed Tatius down the trail. By the time they reached the villa, Nikolaos and Dacia had prepared a bowl of peach juice. Tatius set the dog down on the ground. Nikolaos took a cup and slowly poured juice down the dog's throat. Pup licked and swallowed. Nikolaos gave him more juice. Then Pup voluntarily opened his massive jaws opened as the tutor poured in more juice.

Pup got up feebly and stood wobbling on his powerful legs. Tatius buried his face in the dog's shoulder whispering, "Pup, Pup, Pup." Then Tatius placed his arms under the big dog's front and back legs, hefted him up, and carried him into the villa.

Secundus led Argolicus and his tutor back out into the villa's garden under the plane tree. "It's time for a bit of wine," he said, "Dacia, wine." The girl came out with a tray full of cups and an urn and placed them on the small table.

As Secundus poured, Tatius came into the garden to join them followed by a tottering Pup. "Your Sublimity, your slave saved the dog's life. I know he is just a farm dog, but I care for that dog."

"Nikolaos knows many things about plants and animals. We were fortunate he was here," Argolicus said. Then without preamble, he asked, "Where is your mother, Livilla Valerius?"

Tatius and Secundus looked at each other and shrugged. Then Tatius said, "I will find her," and headed inside.

Secundus sipped at his wine, stopped, reached for another cup, and offered one to Nikolaos who was once again standing under the plane tree. "Thank you, Nikolaos. We are grateful for your knowledge, and your skill."

Nikolaos accepted the wine cup with a slight bow.

"Oh, oh, oh. Your Sublimity, I hear your fabulous slave saved Pup," the widow Livilla said as she slid onto a chair under the tree next to Secundus, fiddled with the neck of her tunic, tipped her chin down and looked up at Argolicus with a smile.

Tatius sat stroking Pup's head as he sipped his wine.

"He did. But I must ask you if you are ready to ride."

"Ride? I don't understand." She posed her chin over her shoulder, trying hard to look winsome.

"Oh, I think you do," Argolicus said.

Tatius and Secundus looked puzzled. Secundus asked, "Why would Mother ride with you?"

"Because of that rose-laurel over there in the corner of your garden."

Livilla fluttered her hands in the air as she gave another coquettish smile. "The rose-laurel, it's lovely with the pink flowers and the silvery leaves. They grow down by the creek. I planted this one when it was young."

"Exactly," Argolicus said. "You planted the rose-laurel. You know the plants in your garden. You supervise the use of the herbs. Dacia uses them to cook at your suggestion."

"Yes," Livilla said. Her hands had stopped fluttering, and the girlish look faded from her eyes.

"And from time to time, you, yourself, pick the herbs, yes?"

Livilla swallowed, looking at Argolicus with a furrowed brow. "Yes, from time to time."

"And one time, a time when you'd had enough of your

husband's bullying and philandering, you picked the flowers from the rose-laurel."

Tatius and Secundus looked at their step-mother. She looked around at all of them, her face suddenly sallow. Her winsomeness disappeared as her shoulders sagged.

"I did," she said. "I did. I picked the flowers, and ground them in the mortar, and took the juice and added it to his wine. I heard him with Dacia. I couldn't...he...I'd had enough." She looked at her stepsons. "You understand, I'd had enough. We could live here comfortably without him."

Secundus pulled back. "Mother, what are you saying?"

"I'm saying enough. Enough. It looked like apoplexy. Who would know? If it weren't for that dog, nobody would know."

Tatius put down his wine cup, stood up, walked to Livilla and slapped her. "You! You gave him poison? Our father? Now I know I was correct to want you to go." He turned to Argolicus.

"There's no need to take her. I will gladly take her myself."

Argolicus looked at the garden and the villa and thought about the farm. A seasonal peach harvest and now the *liquamen* factory did not make these men rich. "And you will pay the Governor with what? He doesn't know law. He isn't a magistrate. And what could he do that you couldn't do yourself? You can resolve this with your original solution. Let her be gone."

Livilla collapsed on the ground. "No. I have nothing. How will I live? You, yourself, told me this morning I have nothing." Then she wailed, "I have no place to go!"

"Causing more pain for your stepsons is not a just solution. For a noble, you would be exiled or put to death. For your situation, the only result would be your stepsons feeding the coffers of the Governor Venantius so he could take on a private matter."

Secundus cried out, "Mother! I thought you were a mother to me."

Livilla, sprawled on the ground, didn't answer. "I've no place. No one," she moaned.

Argolicus gestured to Nikolaos. "We'll leave you to your family matters," he said to them.

Tatius turned to Argolicus. "You Sublimity, before you go…"

❧

It was late evening when Argolicus found his mother in her room, combing out her hair.

"Mother, your Widow Valerius was not a good woman. I'll tell you in a minute. First, I think you need to know, we have a new asset."

Amalina looked up as Nikolaos entered with Pup. She put down the comb and leaned toward the dog.

- Ω -

GLOSSARY

Acacian division - The prelate of Constantinople, Acacius, advised the Byzantine emperor Zeno to issue the Henotikon edict in 482 C.E., in which Nestorius and Eutyches were condemned, the twelve chapters of Cyril of Alexandria accepted, and the Chalcedon Definition ignored. This effort to shelve the dispute over the Orthodoxy of the Council of Chalcedon eventually came to nothing but was not ended until 319 C.E.

Atrium - The formal reception room at the front of a Roman home. Members of the family received guests here. The roof had an opening in the middle so the room was exposed to weather. Most atriums also had a pool of water in the middle which captured rain.

Civilitas- A concept of civility and fairness proclaimed by King Theoderic, to bear on all relations between and among people under his rule.

Civitas - The Roman law that bound citizens together in a common agreement binding all Roman citizens.

Garum - A sauce made by fermenting salted fish offal for

months in the open air. Considered a delicacy and common on all tables.

Palla - A large shawl (approximately 12 feet by 5 feet) originally worn by men and women. At the time of the story, a garment worn by women.

Peristylum - A large room at the back of a Roman home. The opening in the roof was larger than that of the atrium. The area was decorated with plants and flowers, often a fountain, and was a family gathering place.

Salutorium - The official reception room for a bishop. Furnishings were sparse except for the bishop's chair. Visitors stood while the bishop sat.

Triclinium - The dining room. Furnished with tables set in the shape of a U. Diners reclined on benches, often padded, to eat. A diner would lean on an elbow to reach food with the opposite hand.

ENJOY THIS BOOK? YOU CAN MAKE A BIG DIFFERENCE.

Thank you for reading *Argolicus Mysteries Collection*.

You wouldn't be here if you didn't like a good mystery and diving into another time.

Building a relationship with my readers is the very best thing about writing.

Reviews are the most powerful tools in my arsenal when it comes to getting attention to my books. Much as I'd like to, I don't have the financial muscle of a big New York publisher. I can't take out full-page ads or put posters on subways.

(Not yet, anyway.) But I have something more powerful and effective than that, and those publishers would kill to get their hands on.

A committed and loyal bunch of readers. Honest reviews of my books help bring them to the attention of other readers.

If you have enjoyed any one of the Argolicus Mysteries I would be very grateful if you could spend just five minutes leaving a review on the book's review page. It can be as short as you like.

Thank you very much!

Want to learn more about Argolicus? Join the Fans of Argolicus (https://zara-altair.ck.page/e4e920bb2e). You'll receive personal updates on new Argolicus stories and what's happening in my writer world.

ABOUT THE AUTHOR

Zara Altair combines mystery with a bit of adventure in the Argolicus mysteries. The *Argolicus Mysteries Collection* collects the first four stories in one volume. The series of mysteries is based in southern Italy at the time of the Ostrogoth rule of Italy under Theoderic the Great. Italians (Romans) and Goths live under one king while the Roman Empire is ruled from Constantinople. At times the cultures clash, but Argolicus uses his wit, sometimes with help from his tutor Nikolaos, to provide justice in a province far from the King's court.

Zara Altair lives in Beaverton, Oregon. Her approach to writing is to present the puzzle and let Argolicus and Nikolaos find the solution encountering a bit of adventure and some humor in their search. Her stories are rich in historical detail based on years of research.

Stay in Touch
www.zaraaltair.com
zara@zaraaltair.com